RIDING HIGH

ZARA
STONELEY

Published by Sourcebooks Casablanca, an imprint of Sourcebooks, Inc., in
conjunction with Xcite Books Ltd.
P.O. Box 4410, Naperville, Illinois 60567-4410
(630) 961-3900
Fax: (630) 961-2168
www.sourcebooks.com

Originally published in 2012 in the UK by Xcite Books Ltd.

Library of Congress Cataloging-in-Publication data is on file with the publisher.

Printed and bound in the United States of America.
VP 10 9 8 7 6 5 4 3 2 1

To the people who are always there for me,
and the man who inspires me

Prologue

"I'D KILL THE BASTARD if he were my husband."

"Yeah, so would I." Roisin leaned over and sloshed another generous measure of Toby's best scotch into Sam's glass. "If he wasn't already dead."

"Sorry? He's what? For a moment there you said…" For the first time since they'd sat down she actually had Sam's attention. All of it. "Jesus, you did, didn't you?" There was silence for a moment, while Sam peered into her glass as if for inspiration, which, when it came, just had to have been alcohol-induced. "Shit, he didn't—you know, die in the middle of…?"

"Sam!"

"Sorry, it's just I once saw this film where the guy had a heart attack while he was…"

"Sam, will you shut up? I'm so glad my mind doesn't work like yours. It must be scary."

"You don't mean someone…?"

"I wish." Roisin grimaced and took a good gulp from her own glass, which did more than hit the spot; it almost annihilated it. "Well, no, I don't even wish, though it would make it easier." She spluttered as the scotch burned its way down her throat, leaving it dry. No, she couldn't wish him actually dead, even if she was drunk, which was a bit of a bummer. "No, it was just a heart attack, probably too much excitement." She swirled the remaining liquid, watching it crawl up the edge of the glass.

"Wow." Sam gaped at her for a moment. "You don't mean… There wasn't more than one, was there?" Her gaze had switched back to the laptop, which was doing its best to illuminate the whole room.

"Oh yeah, there was more than one." She almost laughed— almost. Even when she was well on the way to drunk it wasn't funny, though, not yet. Maybe in another zillion years or so. And nor had it been the slightest bit funny finding the home movie when she'd been sorting out his office—or, rather, the collection of home movies. Toby, it seemed, was quite a collector.

"So I was almost right the first time. But"—Sam's silences said as much as her words—"it's just I wouldn't have thought that he…"

"Had it in him?"

"Well, um, you know he isn't—he wasn't exactly…" Sam's voice trailed off and she downed her drink in a kind of awed silence, still staring at the frozen image on the laptop.

Roisin had to admit it was kind of mesmerizing, seeing him in glorious Technicolor with a look of uninhibited pleasure on his face. Mesmerizing and weird because it just wasn't—well, it wasn't Toby. The Toby she knew hadn't exactly been stud material; he wasn't hot, or even lukewarm, not even by her standards, which Sam assured her were pretty low. Toby had just been Toby: normal, slightly boring, slightly pompous Toby. Her husband.

And she'd already spent far too many hours staring at him humping away on the screen; she'd only shared the movie because it was easier than trying to explain. She jabbed at the Eject button and the DVD jumped out, clattering with finality onto the table.

Sam gave a guilty start. "Sorry, I just don't know what to say."

Ah, those words you just never think you'll hear, and *voilà*, there they are. In a "you couldn't make it up" type of situation. This was the point when she should be able to press the Rewind button and relive this part of her life.

Damn. She took a more cautious sip of whiskey. "Don't worry, nor do I." It had been one thing to find out that her shit of a husband had been having an affair, or more likely several consecutive affairs, since the day they had taken that long walk down the aisle. Bad enough to see that lousy DVD of the clammy-handed idiot having his silly little cock sucked by some platinum blond with bare boobs that looked like they were about to explode from implant overload. Faintly nauseating to see those long, red talons rake over his puny, pale body. But it was quite another thing, and so, so much worse, that the bastard had had the temerity to drop down dead before she could tell him she knew. That was the bit that really wound her up. That, and the look of pure satisfaction that had been shining on his sweaty face as he'd shot his load all over the poor girl's triple-Ds. She gave a shudder; what a bloody mess. In more ways than one, which should be funny except that right now it was just adding insult to injury. They both stared at the blank screen.

She missed him. That made it worse too.

"So I missed the funeral?"

"Well, I knew you two hated each other"—she smiled at Sam's worried look—"and anyway, you were away, there didn't seem much point in bothering you." Roisin shrugged. "Let's face it, he wasn't exactly Mr. Popular." But she had loved him, or thought she did. Or at least been very fond of him in a fairly polite, distant kind of way. Like her mom had been fond of her dad. Shit, had she really been so stupid? Talk about the sins of your fathers…

"Oh, it wouldn't have been a bother." Sam grinned lopsidedly, which could have been the whiskey or it could have been confusion. "So what now? Are you going to carry on with this place?"

She stared blankly at Sam. The million-dollar question: what now? "I dunno, really." The last dregs of the whiskey parted company with the bottle. "The library of home porn is just about all he left me. Seems like he spent all the money."

"You're kidding me? But I thought you were loaded."

"So did I."

"That's a helluva lot of home movies, isn't it?"

"A helluva lot." She swirled her glass, letting the fumes drift up until they caught the back of her throat and she had an excuse for the fact her eyes were watering. She'd thought money hadn't been a problem; she'd thought lots of things. A new life hadn't featured on the list.

"You're better off without him, Ro, honest. You know what you've got to do?"

"Surprise me."

Sam grinned. "Whatever you fucking want, girl. In fact"—she leaned forward conspiratorially—"I'd have wild, crazy monkey sex with the first guy you bump into."

"I know you would, you do that anyway." Roisin grinned back, hooked her legs over the arm of the chair. "But knowing my luck, it would be the horny pig farmer up the road and not some handsome sex god."

"Well yeah, but you know horny can beat handsome hands

down. If the flesh is willing…" She rumpled her pretty face into a leer and thrust her hips forward.

"The one I'm thinking about would need a sack over his head and a good spraying with disinfectant."

"Oh, Ro, you're such a frigid prude."

"And you, Sam, are such a tart."

She stuck her tongue out as Sam hitched her skirt suggestively and blew her a kiss. Drinks with her old school mate hadn't been on the menu for a long time; too long, not since she'd gotten married and they'd drifted their separate ways. Roisin toward slightly staid coupledom, Sam striding determinedly along the rude and raunchy road of singledom.

Well, she wasn't sure about jumping the first man she saw, but at least burying Toby had been the first step, which, she had to concede, wasn't an option a lot of cheated women were given.

Chapter 1

Roisin banged the half-empty bottle of scotch back down on the shelf abruptly and watched the other bottles jump in sympathy. Move on. Yeah. Move on, that's what she needed to do, once she worked out how to do it without any money. And once she worked out how to get that image of a wanking Toby out of her head.

"Whoa, is that the way you treat all your good scotch?"

Roisin froze as the deep voice hit and sent a tingle straight down her spine. All the way down to its base, then it spread out into a kind of warm shimmer between her thighs that made her breath hitch. That shouldn't be possible, and nor should the rush of dampness straight to her panties. She was supposed to be Miss Frigid, wasn't she? Not Miss Jump On The First Man You See And Have Wild Monkey Sex.

"Or are you just heavy-handed with the cheap stuff?" The low reverberation of a male chuckle made her nipples tighten in anticipation. Shit. Her grip tightened on the bottle; she'd be quite happy just standing here clenching her pussy until she came, except she couldn't. It was a bar, and she was the only person behind it, and he was a customer. Getting off on his voice wasn't an option.

So she turned around. Mistake.

Roisin could have sworn she could see every one of his toned abs through that fitted shirt, or maybe it was just her overactive imagination filling in the gaps. But the strong, broad chest was real, and so were the brown Labrador eyes that matched the voice perfectly and should have had a sanity warning attached.

Standing with your mouth open while you're running your tongue over your lips and teeth as though you want to run it over him is so not a good look. But she couldn't help it, even though this stranger was not her type. He was definitely—no, more than definitely not her type. He had a suit on, and she didn't like suits, didn't like brash City types. She liked them even less than she liked horny pig farmers. Well, maybe not if they looked like this.

"Hey." He grinned and started to tug his tie off, undoing the top button of his shirt with a tanned, strong hand as if he was more comfortable out of his clothes, the dark eyes never leaving her.

Oh my God, please don't show any more of your body. Slowly, he rolled up his shirtsleeves. Shit. "You look like you need a drink as much as I do right now." He ran his hand through a mass of unruly dark curls, his head tipped to one side, all beguiling man-boy.

Oh yes, she needed a drink. A strong drink. Okay, she was pretty sure she was staring, staring at him like he was prime steak and she hadn't eaten for days. But it wasn't food she was hungry for, not really. Just looking at him reminded her she hadn't had sex for longer than she wanted to remember. In fact, when it came to sex she was a one-woman famine zone. And she'd definitely never before had, or even thought she wanted, a taste of a man who looked quite like this. And he was right: she needed a drink. And she needed to operate her mouth and say something, instead of mentally licking her lips. God, she hoped it was just mentally.

"Um—I mean, yes, I'm only rough with the cheap stuff." Bugger.

"Ah, looks like I'll have to watch my manners, then." He grinned, a big, dirty grin that said he wasn't planning on watching his manners at all. "Unless I want some rough handling." He was close. Too close, far too close. Sending a strong whiff of maleness in her direction. It could have been aftershave; it could have been hormones, but who cared? It was making her feel seriously randy.

"Yes." Which came out all squeaky. Calm. She just had to be calm and relaxed. "What do you fancy?"

He leaned forward a bit, resting his tanned, muscled forearms on the bar, and caught her arm with his thumb, which didn't help at all. "Well"—his laugh rumbled around her—"seeing as you're asking…"

Christ, she must be able to stop blushing, and she really must be able to say something that didn't sound like she was asking permission to jump him. Except she was asking, wasn't she?

Talking to men had never been her strong point, and it would seem that even at thirty it still wasn't. Maybe five long years of a soulless marriage and the type of sex that made your eyes water for all the wrong reasons had made her even worse at it.

She shifted her arm nervously away. This wasn't how she normally behaved at all, but he was just so sexy, or she was sex-starved and desperate. Or both.

"I think I better…" She edged back, trying to ignore the way his gaze raked over her body, but her nipples were peaking in response, and her stomach was coiled with a fierce kind of hunger. She straightened a glass that didn't need it; what was she even doing here? Just for once she'd thought a change of scene would do her good, help her forget the disaster she once called a life. And it might have done if Mr. Sex-on-Legs hadn't walked in.

"I'll go for the bitter if you promise to pull it nice and slow." He grinned. "No rough handling." He shifted back a bit on the bar stool, and she remembered she knew how to breathe.

"Fine, I promise to pull it exactly how it's supposed to be pulled." There must have been the teacher's edge to her voice from the slightly amused look he shot her, but it was something she couldn't help; that instinctive warning when somebody was telling her how to suck eggs. Even if he was making her all gooey inside, which proved she wasn't a completely lost cause when it came to men, and almost made her smile.

He reached out just as she put the beer down, so that for a brief moment his hand covered hers, sending another shiver of something that really wasn't good straight through her body. "I can't persuade you to stop for a sec and have a drink with me?" He glanced pointedly around the deserted pub. "Join me on the wrong side of the bar, seeing as you're not exactly run off your feet?"

"Well…"

"Just for one before you shut up shop for the night? I promise I won't bite."

Biting might be good. She bit down on her bottom lip to stop the grin that twitched at her insides, and refilled her glass. "I take it you're used to somewhere a bit livelier than this?" She wasn't fishing, not really. She didn't care who he was or where he came from. She was going to accept him for the gift she was starting to realize he was.

"Ever so slightly. I don't think anywhere in London can compete with this, not even the morgue."

Ah, London. She'd been right, City type. So what was he doing here in Hicksville?

"This corner of Cheshire isn't exactly the bright lights, though you should see it on market day." Pulling the stool farther from him looked a bit obvious, so she guessed she'd just have to settle for unnervingly close.

"You do sometimes get people in here, then?" He shifted in closer, his gaze intent on hers.

"Yup, now and again, though probably not what you're used to."

"It has its attractions, this corner of Cheshire, even without lots of people." She tried to ignore his finger as it traced a slow line of heat from her elbow right down to her wrist, tried to ignore the almost indiscernible pressure from his fingertips that was sending a flutter of something illicit straight between her thighs. "Bright lights aren't everything, you know."

"Really?" She tried to control the squeak.

"Really." The heat of his thigh against hers burned its way straight to her pussy, building up the ache that had started the moment he had touched her.

"You're just, um, passing through, then?" Just so she knew, had it straight in her head.

"I'm just passing through." He nodded, close enough for her to feel his warm breath caressing her neck.

So she was rubbish at interrogation; at least that was firmly established. No one just passed through this place; it wasn't as though there was a motorway running through it, or anything else, for that matter. But if she sat and had a drink with him, if she sat and let him flirt…At least he'd be gone tomorrow. When she might be regretting it and wishing she'd stayed at home and finished the chocolates and book, in that order.

Saul Mathews watched the barmaid pour him a second pint. He wasn't that bothered about another drink, but he didn't want to give her a chance to skip off and busy herself doing nothing again. Normally he did his best to avoid talking to the locals when he did a job like this. He came in, made his assessment, and left. No whimsical fancies about the people or the place, no emotions, just decisions based on clinical facts. But he hadn't been able to ignore her; she was just there, inescapable, and when those soulful green eyes had locked with his, it had been an invitation he couldn't ignore. Even if she didn't seem to realize she was issuing an invitation at all.

It was late, and the motorway traffic on the way up had moved at the speed of a funeral dirge, which had cocked up his schedule completely. If it hadn't, he'd have done what he came to do and been heading back to the safety of the city already. Instead he was stuck in the middle of nowhere, and he needed a room for the night. Which he should be asking her about.

He'd checked out the stable yard that was the purpose for his long drive; it had been shrouded in dark, the type of black you only found in the depths of the countryside these days. And the countryside, it seemed, shut up shop when it went dark. So he'd headed for the nearest thing to civilization for the night. There was only one pub in the village, which was as deserted as the rest of the place. Apart from a girl with a body he wanted to touch, lips he wanted to kiss, and a voice that he wanted to hear talking dirty. He knew he shouldn't, but he wanted her. Really wanted her. And her body was sending out the type of signal that said the feeling was mutual.

It wasn't just that she was sexy, though she was, very sexy in an understated, comfortable in her body type of way. It was the way she looked at him, the undercurrent of need as though she wanted him but hadn't realized it yet. That alluring mix of innocence and sensuality was turning him on something rotten. That was how mermaids did it, wasn't it? Lured men to their deaths? But all life had been offering him lately seemed to be blatant, and blatant had gotten boring.

Saul took a deep swallow of the bitter, letting the malt envelop his taste buds; he traced a finger through the cool, damp condensation on the glass and wondered what she tasted like. He couldn't remember the last time he'd had a one-night stand; he thought he'd grown out of those. And something told him that this girl didn't do casual either. Normally. But tonight she needed him. Her body knew, even if her brain hadn't caught up. And his had been short circuited; he didn't even know her name yet.

"I'm Saul, by the way. Saul Mathews." He held out a hand. For a second, it looked like she was going to give him the brush-off, then she grasped it with slender, soft fingers that had a surprisingly firm touch, sending a zing straight to his crotch, a zing that must have registered in his eyes, because she bit on the full bottom lip that had been tantalizing him for what seemed a long time.

"Roisin." She smiled for the first time, and her small, serious face colored in a blush that he could imagine spreading down over her body. His cock started to twitch in response, way too early for comfort.

"Nice name." He didn't let go of the fingers.

"You can call me Rosie if you like, people find it easier." She looked at him, with a mix of apology and challenge. And Saul did challenges, not apologies.

"Easier maybe, but not as sexy, Roisin." He rolled her name

over on his tongue again, brushing her hand with his thumb, watching mesmerized as her nipples pebbled in response. "Fancy a walk in the fresh air when you've finished here?"

"Sure."

The air was fresh all right, but it wasn't exactly what Roisin fancied. She wanted him, right here, right now. Even though wanting was dangerous; something she'd managed to avoid most of her life. She could have blamed the feeling of light-headedness on the second glass of wine, or on the cool, fresh air. But it wasn't either. It was need, want, the unexpected thrill of anticipation that was running through her. She'd never lived dangerously; her life had been satisfyingly organized and well run. She seemed to have skipped the "live life on the edge" bit. Until now, when she suddenly felt like she didn't have anything left to lose. And she didn't have to do anything for anyone else again. This was just for her. Having wild, uninhibited sex with a stranger had never been an item on her wish list, but suddenly it seemed to have shot to pole position. And she was fairly sure some fairy godmother was waving a wand about for all she was worth.

"Cold?" He ran a finger over the shiver of goose bumps down her arms, and draped his jacket over her shoulders, pulling her closer toward a warm, firm body, sending a new shiver through her that had nothing to do with the cold.

"Roisin." The way he said her name, so deliberately, made her look up. The brown eyes locked on to hers, and then his head dropped closer and all she was aware of was his lips. Strong, firm lips that were gently parted. She turned fully, closed the slight gap he had left between them, the invitation that he was offering. The instant she did, his hands slipped under the jacket, fastened around her waist. A soft moan slipped from her as the warmth of his touch sent a new rush of dampness straight between her thighs. It was dark at the back of the pub, only the lights from a room on the first floor above casting a glimmer over him. It was even darker in the shadow of the wall he pushed her against.

"How the hell's a man supposed to resist you?" His words breathed against her mouth for the briefest moment, then his lips came down hard in a bruising kiss that made her gasp. As her lips parted automatically, his tongue skated over her teeth.

He tasted of arousal, of lust, as his tongue explored farther into her mouth, playing with hers until her body started to respond, her hips shifting closer to him, each touch sending a new jangle of awareness through her. She reached up, moaning as she tangled her fingers in the soft hair that had been tempting her since she'd first seen him; held him close as he sucked on her tongue in a way that mingled pain and pleasure. One large hand cupped her bum, forcing her between his slightly parted thighs so she could feel his hard cock trapped between them.

She rocked her hips, shifting and sliding against him, desperate to feel his heat against her slit. His deep groan in her mouth sent a new flood of juices between thighs that were already damp.

She dimly heard a whimper, knew it must be her, as his hand scorched its way under her skirt, high up the inside of her trembling thigh, setting off an involuntary shudder as his long fingers edged under the lace of her panties. A gasp filled her throat as he brushed against oversensitized skin, and she wriggled her hips apart to help him ease farther in, moaning louder as he traced along her slit before slipping one finger deep inside her slickness. God, that was good; she'd stopped trying to kiss him, stopped trying to do anything except hang on to him as his finger explored her sopping cunt.

"Shit, you're so wet, so gorgeous…" He twisted his hand, rubbing against her engorged clit for a moment before slipping a second finger inside. "Is that good?" His dark eyes melted into hers as he pressed his thumb firmly against her swollen bud, and then he started to play his fingers against a G-spot that she could swear was swelling at every stroke.

She would have said yes if she'd been able to speak instead of pant, but she could feel it coming, feel it so close. She moaned, tipped her hips, rocking against his hand desperately as the distant tremor in her pussy turned into an urgent throb. "Please." And he knew exactly what to do to tip her over the edge, to release the waves of spasms so they broke over her with a sudden rush of intensity, rocking her whole body. "Shit." She clutched at his shoulder, digging her nails in as he took her mouth, his tongue hard against hers, his hand tight in her hair, tipping her head back farther as his thumb massaged and his fingers gently played with her cunt until every last tremor of the orgasm was spent.

"I think you needed that." The lazy smile clutched at her throat as he slowly drew back and slipped his fingers out, tracing down the inside of her thigh, coating it with her own juices. Then he gently stroked the back of his hand down her cheek with a promise that made her tremble. "Are you ready to see what comes next?"

Swallowing hard, she waited for the world to stop rocking. "You mean there's more?" Shit, she was still seeing stars.

"Oh yeah, plenty more." He grinned.

"Ouu." Roisin grinned back. Wow, as fairy godmothers went, this one had done her proud. "What the hell are we doing standing here, then?" She grabbed his hand and practically dragged him through the back door of the pub and up the narrow staircase that led to the rooms her brother called home.

—⁓—

"You are just so fuckable."

She'd only made it halfway up the stairs when his hand came down over hers on the banister, stopping her in her tracks.

"Hey." She half turned, but he was hard up against her, his other arm snaking out around her waist.

"Stop right there, darling." His soft voice in her ear sent a warning tingle as he pulled her unresisting hand from the rail and pushed her slightly forward so that she had to reach both arms out to the step to stop herself sprawling.

Cold air rushed over her bum as he flipped her skirt up high over her back, one hand holding her firm, the other pushing between her still-damp thighs to ease them farther apart. Christ, he wasn't going to…? One yank and he'd ripped her panties down to her ankles. He buried his face between her legs, nuzzling his way toward a pussy she knew was wet and glistening.

Fuck. She moaned, biting into her hand as his tongue instantly found her swollen clit, making her pussy clench, making her claw at the stairs as he moved along her folds, opening her up to his mouth. His groan echoed inside her as he lapped at her juices. She parted her thighs even farther, her stomach and arms starting to tremble. He needed to be deeper inside her; she needed that tongue to explore her pussy in the same way it had explored her mouth. She desperately lifted her bum higher until she was balanced on her toes, rocking as he licked and probed.

Last time a man had gone down on her it had seemed like a duty, like he was licking where he felt he should, sucking for the amount of time that was reasonable, a warm-up for the shag that was his real focus of pleasure. But this was different. Far, far different. Saul was reacting to every tremble of her thighs, every moan and whimper that escaped her lips, sucking, stroking, nibbling, lapping up the juices that flowed from her, sucking her clit gently, then harder as his fingers slipped inside her. One finger, two, three; she wasn't sure what he was doing anymore as she rocked against his mouth, his hand, each thrust and stroke building up until she couldn't bear it any longer. And then she didn't have to. The orgasm hit her, her pussy clenching and releasing in a way she couldn't have stopped if her life had depended on it, and she knew she was babbling as she clutched helplessly at the stair carpet.

―――

Unlocking the door was hard because her hand wouldn't stop trembling, partly from the orgasm, but so much more from the anticipation of what was going to happen next.

"Here." Impatience took over and he took the key from her, opening the door and pushing her in, kicking it shut behind them. Her legs still shook from the orgasm that was melting her insides as he spun her around and pushed her back hard against the wall. She reached out, her hands curling instinctively into his hair as he pushed his hard body against hers, trapping her. She hadn't yet seen him without clothes, but she felt like she knew every molded inch of him. She tried to pull his head closer but this time he didn't move, kept the same distance.

"Kiss me, please." Her voice had a husky, unfamiliar edge to it, close to desperation. She'd be begging soon and she didn't care.

"Oh no." He shook his head and his mouth curled at the corners. "We're doing this at my speed, or it'll be over far too soon."

She could hear a catch in his voice, a harsh edge of control that hadn't been there before. Then, before she could react, he caught both her wrists and pinned them up above her head, transferring them into one large hand so he had one free. Slowly, he traced a finger down her cheek, her neck, smiling as she shivered with anticipation. He traced lower, down the center of her chest, into the dip between her breasts. He paused for the slightest moment before covering one breast with his hand, rubbing gently until her nipple hardened against his palm. "The perfect handful." He squeezed, and shards of need shot straight down her stomach, to a pussy that was already hot, already bathed in her juices. She shifted her hips, trying to relieve some of the tension, and he gave a low, throaty laugh that echoed through her body.

Slowly, he unbuttoned her blouse, tightening his grip slightly on her wrists, stretching her body so her breasts were lifted, switching every nerve ending to "on." His fingers drifted over the delicate lace of her bra, teasing, tempting in a way that made her body shimmy as she desperately tried to get closer to him. He paused, glancing up at her flushed face before beginning to lick slowly and deliberately around the covered nipple, massaging the hard bud until it peaked, until frissons of need shot down to her stomach, making her muscles clench, tightening her stomach, tightening her pussy. His mouth closed around her breast, sucking until she was whimpering with need.

"Saul, please…"

Suddenly he bit hard, causing a jolt of pain that made her cry out in surprise. A new spasm of excitement shot straight to her cunt.

Firm fingers pushed the fabric of her bra under her breasts, holding her steady as he took the soft flesh of her breast deeper into his mouth, his tongue flicking gently, soothing, playing with her until she felt she couldn't bear it any longer. She moaned, and he sucked harder. She knew her hips were swaying in time with his suckling, knew that each movement brought her orgasm closer, and then he took his mouth away, and the cold air hit her damp skin with fresh, tingling sensation.

Roisin swayed as she watched him, feeling abandoned without the touch of his mouth, his hands. He unbuckled his belt and stepped out of his trousers, rolling a condom onto a hard-on that jutted impatiently out. She ran her tongue expectantly over her lips and he smiled.

"Another time, babe. Right now I need to be inside you. I need to have you, now." *Now*. The firm way he said it sent a new prickle of awareness straight to her already throbbing pussy and she reached a hand down between her warm, damp thighs instinctively. Now wasn't soon enough; he'd given her more foreplay than she'd had in a lifetime and all it had done was make her greedy.

"I've got something better than your fingers for that sweet pussy." He pulled her closer to him, kissing her briefly, his tongue skimming her lips, before turning her toward the arm of the chair. Her legs shook as he pushed her forward. One second was all it seemed to take for him to shove her skirt roughly up and push her legs wider apart. She felt his firm thumbs on her buttocks, felt them press down in her crack, and then his hard, jutting cock was against her. He was breathing hard as he teased her wet cunt, brushing his cock up and down, each stroke opening her up, making her more desperate to feel him deep inside her. He reached around to cup one of her breasts in a capable hand, tweaking her nipple as she pushed her bottom back impatiently against him. His fingers tightened painfully on her, making her yelp, and as she did, he thrust. One deep thrust that buried him to the hilt and made her cry turn into a scream of surprise. His hand moved from her breast down to her hip, gripping firmly as he withdrew slightly and thrust again, and this time she moaned. Both his hands held her firm as she clutched at the fabric of the cushions, lifting her bottom higher as he pounded into her, pushing back so that she could hear his balls slapping against her as the pain of pleasure started to build up inside her again.

"Hang on, baby, hang on." She could hear the tension in his voice, feel his fingers tighten as she fought the need to come. She couldn't stand it anymore, needed him to push her over the edge. He was growing harder, bigger inside her with each thrust, the rasp of her nipples against the fabric of the chair winding her body up tighter. "Now." It was a guttural moan.

She knew. He hadn't needed to say it; she knew he was about to come, could feel the surge, and as she let go, so did he. And Roisin suddenly discovered just how good shagging a stranger could be.

———

Roisin stretched and flung out an arm. Then realization hit her. One, it wasn't her bed; two, she ached in places she didn't know she had; and three, the sheets next to her were rumpled. Very rumpled. As though there had been an orgy in them.

Shit. She groaned and rolled over on her front, burying her face in the pillow. Which smelled unmistakably of male. Double shit.

She rolled back over on her side and opened an eye. The pillow next to her had a definite dip in it. A head-shaped type of dip. But, luckily, no head. Which got her sitting bolt upright, and grabbing the sheet to cover her boobs, just in case.

Oh fuck, what had happened to her? What had she just done?

Oh yeah, she'd had sex. Lots of sex, in a way she'd never imagined before. Wild monkey sex, as Sam would have called it, with the first man she had bumped into.

She flopped back on the bed, staring at the ceiling. If she shut her eyes maybe it would all go away. Toby might only have been gone a matter of months, but it was much longer than that since she'd had sex, and even then that had been polite, "would you mind terribly if I come?" kind of sex. Which meant maybe Sam had been right—both about her being a prude and about wild monkey sex being the answer. Except now she wasn't too sure.

The only good part was that he'd gone, which cut out the early morning embarrassment, the "what the hell do I say?" bit, and meant she could pretend everything was normal. But, if she was honest, that didn't really feel that good at all now. Why the fuck had he been such a rude bastard that he'd bolted; had she been that bad? Maybe she had been frigid.

She glanced at the clock just to make sure, but yep, it was only six a.m. She always woke early, even, it seemed, after the type of shag-you-senseless sex that left you out for the count, and right now she had to get going. Not lie here clutching the sheets and trying to work out just how the hell she'd managed to get her leg over his shoulder like that. She wasn't sure "leg over" was supposed to mean that.

Bugger, she'd never catch up if she didn't stop reliving her exploits and get her butt into gear. Which was why she shouldn't have stayed in town; she should have gone home like she usually did. She winced and swung her feet out of bed, putting a hand out to feel the covers where he'd been. Still warm. Still with the slightest scent of male muskiness left behind to tease her. No, it was better he'd taken off. Avoided any awkwardness, even if it stung her pride a bit, which was all it was. Which was stupid. After all, it hadn't exactly been a mistake, but nor was it supposed to be the start of anything. It had been one night of lust, of releasing the desperate need he had wakened in her. One shag. One "start your life all over again" shag.

From now on, things had to go back to normal, though what if she couldn't get back to normal? She tugged at her bottom lip with her teeth. Maybe she'd have to buy a vibrator, or something. Fuck. And she really must stop swearing like this; Toby would be horrified, so would her father. Except they weren't here to care, were they, so who gave a…?

She turned on the shower and let the water hit her. Forget it. Forget him. Go. Back. To. Normal. Her hands drifted down, soaped between her thighs, and caressed the soft, swollen skin of her pussy. She closed her eyes, remembered the feel of his hands, of his probing fingers easing her lips apart and slipping deep inside…

The smell of coffee hit her first. Then the sight of newly showered male. Large male, in a small kitchen. Making it impossible to keep the kind of distance she needed.

"Oh, you're still here." That sounded nasty and kind of ungrateful, which she wasn't normally.

"Sure am. Coffee?" He gave her a lopsided, semiapologetic

smile. "Look, I'm sorry, but I'm afraid I've got to split in a minute."
He didn't look the type of man who was ever really sorry about anything. His hair was still damp from his shower and for a moment she
wanted to reach out and push a stray curl back into place. Instead,
she sat down, firmly on her hands.

"Coffee's good, thanks. Um, well, it was nice to meet you,
Saul." At least she could remember his name, which was good,
wasn't it? Maybe it would have been better if she'd come down to
find him gone, though, because she didn't know what was supposed to come next.

He raised an eyebrow. "Nice to meet me?"

She shrugged. "What am I supposed to say? Thanks for the
shag?" He gave a short laugh that made her feel even more stupid,
and only succeeded in getting her back up. Would he have pre-
ferred her to say "good pounding"? Did "shag" just nowhere near
cover it? "Well, what's the difference between me saying that and
you rushing off to avoid the early morning embarrassment?"

"I wasn't rushing off to avoid embarrassment."

"Well, it would help if you were."

"Sorry?" He looked bemused.

"Hey, forget it." She took a sip of scalding coffee and winced as
it brought tears to her eyes. "Please, can you just…" This was worse
than she thought it would be. "I thought you were in a hurry?"

"Fine, if that's what you want." He shrugged, picked up his
jacket. He was obviously better at this than she was. "If I'm passing
by this way again…?"

"I don't think so, do you?" She had a life to sort out, and this
time she was going to do it on her own; any screwups were going to
be all her own work. She held the cup of coffee up to hide the way

she was sure her lips were wobbling. "It was very nice, though."
From the look he threw her way, that hadn't been quite the right
thing to say. Oh, sod him. He'd not find her again anyway, even if
he did "pass this way." If he thought she was some handy barmaid
on tap like the beer, he was wrong. The place was her brother's,
and she'd only stepped in to cover for him because he'd been desperate and she hadn't really had any reason to say no. And she'd
thought a change was as good as a rest, or something like that. Not
that she'd had a rest.

She could already feel her thighs heating up at the thought,
delicious warmth flooding a pussy that was still swollen from his
attentions. And she couldn't deny it was a nice thought, a repeat
performance. She felt her stomach clench, and other parts; more
than a nice thought, in fact. But not a sensible thought.

"It was good. Um, thanks." Did you say thanks after a man
had shagged you senseless? Or was that a bit crass?

He was giving her that quizzical look. "Yeah, Roisin." He'd
dropped a tone, was rolling her name on his tongue as though
he was eating her. Had gone back briefly to the man she'd seen
last night, which wasn't good. Not good at all. For a moment, he
looked like he was going to step closer, touch her, but he must
have seen the shuttered look that she knew was on her face. "You're
right, it was good. And thank you too."

He nodded slowly, his lips tightening, then he shoved his
hand into his trouser pocket and was gone, jacket slung over his
shoulder, his tie hanging loose. Looking just like he had when he'd
walked into the bar last night. Sexy as hell.

The sound of the door snapping shut echoed through the flat.
Yeah, it had been good. In fact, it had been good enough to make

her forget all about Toby, his women, and the way he'd spent every last penny of their money.

Saul had never been into horses. Riding, yes; horses, no. But right now, watching the slim, strong thighs squeezing firmly against the side of the black horse, he had a sudden desire to get into jodhpurs. Big time. He watched for a moment as the pair moved gracefully around the arena, the rider sitting perfectly upright, moving effortlessly in time with the horse. His gaze moved up to the small, perfect, bouncing breasts, the thick, red curls down her back, and suddenly the picture came together. It was the final piece of the jigsaw that sent a jolt of recognition straight through his body. Straight to his cock. Roisin.

She didn't seem to notice him the first time she cantered past, but then she lost tempo for a moment and the next time around came to a perfect halt feet away, scattering rubber and sand over his feet. And she looked angry. Flushed and angry. That look sent another dart of longing straight to his groin, and it took considerable control to stop himself from dragging her down off that goddamned horse and shagging her right then and there in the dirt.

"How did you find me?" Roisin glared at him. Mind-blowing sex was one thing, but was it good or bad when your supposedly once in a lifetime one-night stand turns up again hours later? Though she couldn't exactly say "You're my one and only one-night stand, now bugger off and stop spoiling things," could she? Or could she?

He shrugged and looked almost apologetic. "I'm sorry, I know this sounds bad, but I didn't find you. I, er, wasn't looking for you."

He didn't really look sorry; he was grinning, and from where she stood it looked like his cock was straining at his zipper as though expecting a repeat performance of last night. She felt the heat hit her cheeks, and forced her gaze back up to meet his.

He glanced down at the sheet of paper he was holding. "I'm actually looking for a Mrs. Grant." The glance turned to a stare, his grin fading. "Mrs."—he paused—"R. Grant." The brown, hangdog eyes shot up to meet her dead-on. "Shit, that's you, isn't it?"

Chapter 2

"Shit, I guess it is." Her voice was soft as she swung her leg over the back of the saddle and slid down off the horse. A slim, toned leg, a thigh that Saul could picture all too clearly naked, wrapped around him.

He swore inwardly and grimaced; this wasn't going the way it was supposed to, which was why he never, ever talked to locals when he was working, and never, ever got involved. "But you live in the town, village, whatever it is." It couldn't be her; he didn't make that type of mistake.

"Nope." She yanked a stirrup up. "I live here." And moved to loosen the girth, her perfect, trim bum only a tempting arm's length away.

If he could only keep his hands to himself this would go fine; he could handle it. Rescue the situation. The sheet of paper started to crumple under his fingers at about the same pace that his balls were tightening. Which wasn't good, because this whole thing wasn't good.

"My brother lives in the village, runs the pub. It's his place."

"I need to talk to you, Roisin."

"Talk, then." She shrugged her small shoulders almost defiantly, still turned away from him. "But don't expect me to listen until I've washed this horse down and put him away. I've got a business to run."

"No, no, I'm sorry but you haven't." Which made him feel like shit, but he didn't know what else to say to get her attention, to stop her fiddling with the bloody horse. "That's just it, Roisin; you don't have a business to run anymore."

~~~

Ah. Or rather, oh fuck. So that was it. She briefly rested her forehead against the hard saddle and breathed in the familiar, comforting smell of warm horse and leather. She'd half expected this—well, more than half, after everything Toby had done. But not him, never in a million years did she expect someone like him. It was supposed to be a sweaty, middle-aged, pompous fool she could hate. Not a man she could still smell warm on her skin.

Whoever was watching over her sure had a warped sense of humor, sending a sex god to shag her senseless one day and strip the rest of her assets the next. That was really taking the piss, nearly enough to make her forget she was about to be dropped in the brown smelly stuff big time. Nearly enough.

"Roisin? Are you okay?" The soft voice reached out and sounded almost sorry, which really stank, because it was a bit like being asked if you had any last requests by the executioner.

"Fine." She let go of the leather strap, which was biting into the palm of her hand, and the horse danced to the side. She forced herself to turn her head and look at him. He hadn't moved a muscle, which spoke a lot for a man in a smart suit who looked as if he thought horses were alien creatures. Most people would have stepped back, away from impatient hooves, but Saul Mathews appeared to have nothing in the way of adrenaline. But plenty of something else; maybe you couldn't have adrenaline and testosterone in equal measures.

He was way too close, his muscled body only thinly disguised by the soft cotton of his perfectly fitted shirt; except she knew exactly what was under that covering now, which made it impossible to ignore. She'd had her hands on it only hours before, a torso that had every muscle defined and perfect, just like a Greek statue. But he wasn't lifeless, cold stone. She could still feel the velvet of his skin; still taste him salty in her mouth. She swallowed. He was staring at her, as though he knew exactly what was whizzing through her head, and her whole body started to react. She clenched her fists, and her teeth.

"So what's that supposed to mean? I haven't got a business?"

He shifted his feet awkwardly on the manège surface, grinding himself deeper into the rubber chips. "I'm sorry, Roisin, but…"

"For heaven's sake, stop saying sorry and just spit it out." This was so unfair, for God's sake; he still smelled of sex and it was turning her on, even though it so seriously shouldn't be.

"Your husband used this place as collateral against some hefty loans." He shoved his hands in his pockets and stood feet astride, as though expecting trouble. "Basically, he'd defaulted on the payments and just before he died the largest debt was called in. You must have known; he must have told you what he was doing."

Nope, he'd not told her when he did it, but yep, she knew she was in trouble. She'd thought they had plenty of money until she'd started to open the letters after Toby had died. She hadn't believed them at first; not until she'd seen that look on the solicitor's face, the look he normally reserved for death and divorce. He'd said he'd get back to her once he'd worked out just how bad it was, fixed a figure on all the debts. Worked out which of the many creditors would be knocking on the door first. But it seemed as though someone had saved him the trouble. Which wasn't a surprise, given the speed he worked at.

She shook her head. "What do you mean the debt was called in?" It might not sound so bad if he spelled it out.

"This place isn't yours anymore. It was sold to my company. As a goodwill gesture we'd agreed that Toby could rent it for a period." His eyes were fixed on her like a hawk, as though he was waiting to see what she would do next. "That period ended just before he died."

Or it could sound worse. "I don't believe you. How could it be before he died? I'd know, wouldn't I?" Maybe if she kept denying it the whole thing would go away.

He shrugged, his lips narrowing in an uncompromising line. "We have written, several times in fact. We've rung him to point out that he is—sorry, was—in breach of our agreement." He sounded stilted, looked awkward. But unrelenting. "He knew, he must have told you."

"It's not mine?" He couldn't really mean what he was saying. This was her home, her business. It couldn't just disappear from under her nose, even if there had been letters. Lots and lots of letters. He was shaking his head slowly, standing waiting for it to sink in, for her to stop blathering on like the village idiot. Her stomach dipped and this time it was nothing to do with lust. "But you can't mean…"

"I'm so—" He stopped the words just in time.

"You're saying it's not mine?"

"It's not yours."

"But I live here."

"Illegally, I'm afraid." His voice was soft.

"My solicitor—"

"It's too late for solicitors; we've gotten past that point."

"I can carry on renting it like Toby agreed with you." Maybe she'd been living in denial; she'd known there was no money left, but she hadn't gotten her head around the fact that this could happen. At least, not yet.

"That was for a finite time, Roisin." He sighed. "It was just a gesture to give your husband some extra time while we assessed the business."

"Assessed it? You mean you're intending to sell it again?" His eyes were guarded. "Oh, I get it, you mean bulldoze it. Is that it? I'm right, aren't I?"

―∞―

Saul didn't want to lie to her. She'd obviously had a belly full of that. "I'm not sure yet what the plan is, but yes, maybe this place will be knocked down." His job was straightforward: he took on a business cheap, identified the saleable assets, then sold the profitable parts to the highest bidder. And sometimes those bits were bulldozed. Or not. "But it's not as if you can afford the rent anyway, can you? I mean, you're not making much money; just pennies."

She was glaring, her whole body tensed for a fight, but he knew she believed him deep down. She knew. "And what was last night about, then? A time filler, or does it turn you on shagging the person you're just about to"—she paused—"shaft in another way?"

"Phew, that's below the belt. That's not fair, and you know it."

"Do I? What do I know, Saul? It seems like you're the one with all the answers."

"Last night was just—it just happened, but believe me if I'd known who you were I would never have even stopped for a drink. It was just bad timing, or good timing if you like." He could feel the corner of his mouth tip and suddenly she looked like she might hit him.

"Oh, fuck off." She flicked the horse's reins over its head and it shied away, almost bumping into him. Which he couldn't blame her for.

"Look, I'm really sorry about this, but I'm not sorry about last night." He stepped up closer, met her glare, because it seemed important that she believed him. Last night hadn't been about business. Last night had been—something else.

"Stop saying you're bloody sorry, unless it's going to change anything."

"It's not going to change anything."

Her eyes were bright and she was gnawing at her lip, but not in the "come and shag me" manner of last night. Which made him feel like shit. Again. "Look, I'll go through the documents with you. That's why I'm here. And if you can come up with some kind of proposal to pay a proper rent on the place then I'll listen."

"I need to sort my horse." She flicked behind the horse with the whip; it stepped forward automatically, brushing past him, leaving a fine coating of sweat-covered hair on his arm. Fine, so she was spoiling for a fight. But he didn't want to fight. Not this time.

He followed slowly behind as she walked toward the stables, studying the property on autopilot. Assessing was something that was second nature to him, even if now it didn't seem right. When he'd pulled into the yard he'd only had time for a quick look around, taking in the tidy but tired air of the place, the look that said it would cost a fortune to update. He grimaced; there was a good-sized house, which he was sure would be in a state, but there were plenty of people around with money who wanted the genuine article, a country estate. Chic, not shabby. The riding stables didn't have much going for them as a business proposition, but the property, the land, did. Which was why he'd bought it. At a knockdown price that he'd thought had meant he couldn't go wrong.

His gaze drifted back to the pert bum and he had a horrible feeling that something, or someone, was about to screw up his plans.

Roisin grabbed a bucket of water angrily. Fuck, he must have known who she was, whatever he said. So she hadn't been just a bed for the night; he'd been weighing her up, softening her up, whatever his tactics were. And she was pissed off. Seriously pissed with him, and even more with herself. She'd fallen straight into the trap he'd set and now he thought it would be simple to waltz in, wave some papers under her nose, and throw her out.

She pulled the saddle off the horse, and dropped it abruptly over the stable door, forcing him to move away. Except he just moved straight back, leaning on the worn leather so that he could watch.

"Frightened I'll run off?"

"Not really. It's just a nice view."

His eyes roamed slowly over her body; it tightened in response, her nipples hardening and a ripple traveling over her stomach and straight between her thighs. Fuck him; two could play at that game. She dipped the sponge into the bucket of water, soaking it so that it dripped as she splashed on to the sweat patch on the horse's back, feeling a rush of water splash back against her chest. She risked a sideways look; his eyes had narrowed slightly. She stretched up, her legs slightly apart, reaching over the horse to sponge the far side, her breasts rubbing against the part that was already wet. Pressing herself against the hot, damp animal, sliding back down, forcing the cold wetness of the skimpy T-shirt against her skin until it was molded to every part of her.

Lather trickled down between her breasts as she dropped the sponge back into the bucket to gather more water; the hardening peaks of her nipples were chafing against the wet material and sending a buzz of expectation straight to her clit. For a second she paused, bent over with her bum in the air, knowing that her tight jodhpurs were like a second skin, clinging to every curve. She liked to wear thongs when she was working; thongs that didn't leave a panty line, that didn't interfere with the freedom she felt when she was riding. That didn't interfere with anything. She could smell her own arousal, smell the juices that were already coating the thin strand of fabric and pooling out inside the tight, revealing cotton of her jodhpurs.

She risked another glance. His knuckles had tightened over the leather saddle, and his darkened eyes were fixed on her bum. She moved to reach under the horse with one hand, sponging slowly down its inner thighs, feeling the trickle of water down her arm, the smell and sensation making her breath come quicker. Keeping her legs taut, she spread her thighs wider, reaching farther under, feeling her whole body sway as she sponged. She paused, shut her eyes. If he came in behind her now, put one large hand between her thighs, caressed her swollen cunt with those knowing fingers, she'd come. If he gripped her hips and shoved her full with that big, hard cock she'd come. Whatever he did would do the trick right now.

Bugger. She snapped out of it, straightened up, and grabbed

the bucket before looking straight at him. His dark eyes burned into her, not a trace of dolefulness, just a look that said any second now he was going to throw her on the straw and fuck her harder and faster than she'd ever been fucked before.

"I'm done now if you want to talk." Her words trembled in her own ears, pure lust. She'd been intent on teasing him, on turning him on and taking some control back, but her whole body was shaking with need as she pulled the stable door firmly behind her and put the bucket down, reaching into it for the sponge. Before she got there his hand was over hers, hard and unyielding.

"Is that what you want?" He drew her up, his fingers biting into her chin as she straightened. One step forward and he was pressed against her so that she could feel the length of his cock, which she could have sworn was even bigger and harder than last night. "Is that what you want to do, talk?" He took another step forward, pushing her roughly so that she was trapped against the wall of the stable block, the hard brickwork against her back cold in contrast to the heat of his body.

The soaking wet sponge was pressed between them, squeezed by the pressure of his body against hers, his hand tightening over the one she clutched it with. Water dripped down between them, soaking his shirt. A rivulet snaked into her cleavage, sending a shiver down her stomach.

"Or do you want something else?" A large, warm hand moved to cradle the side of her face, a hand that was possessive, controlling, giving her no escape route even if she wanted it.

Hard lips came down on hers, and there was none of the gentle touch of last night. This was a harsh demand, instantly rough and bruising, and she opened up to him instinctively. His tongue forced its way into the moist depths of her mouth, eliciting a moan that seemed to come from deep within her as his fingers tightened in her hair. She sucked hard, possessing the only part of him she could, felt him stiffen, and then there was a fresh rush of warmth between her thighs as he forced a knee between her legs, pushing them apart so that he could press his body hard against her, capturing her. A shiver ran through her body as his hips ground against hers, and as he pushed harder the feeling was so intense they could have been naked. She pushed back, tilting her hips so that his dick was pressed just where she needed it, hard against her clit, the heat burning through the thin fabric of his trousers, through the thin tightness of her riding pants. She pushed harder, panting as she felt the muscles deep inside her core start to clench. He dragged his mouth from hers, his fingers in her hair holding her fast against the wall. The pressure eased on her crotch and she mewed out an objection. He smiled, but this was no gentle smile, this was a wolfish smile that spelled out an animal need.

The door of the adjoining stable crashed open as he pushed her in, ricocheting against the wall. It slammed shut behind them, the metallic click of the catch the only sound apart from their shared erratic breathing.

He hooked a foot deftly beneath her legs, sending her sprawling onto the thick bed of straw. "Don't play games with me unless you mean it." His voice was ragged and her nipples tightened against the wet, cold material that clung to her body as he stared down at her. He paused for a minute, giving her time to object, and then he was next to her, his mouth closed around her breast, biting and sucking through the damp covering so it was plastered even tighter against her skin. Cursing, he pulled his mouth away, then dragged at the soaked T-shirt, pulling it roughly over her head, exposing a flimsy lacy bra.

One yank and the delicate material gave way, her breasts spilling out, exposed and ready for his mouth. His lips closed around a nipple already taut with awareness, and then she gasped as firm fingers grasped her crotch, pressing against the warm dampness of her panties.

Roisin reached down, panting, struggling to peel the tight jodhpurs off, needing to feel the heat of his fingers inside her for real, and the instant there was room his hand filled it. He pulled at the lacy thong, the thin fabric tearing as she lifted her hips. His mouth closed tighter around the tightened bud of her nipple, biting, sending a sharp pain of pleasure straight through her as he thrust two fingers deep inside her slick cunt.

She screamed out at the sudden blissful intrusion, fingers tightening convulsively in his hair, twisting deeper as the orgasm shot through her body, bucking her hips with a need she didn't know she had. She was still pulsing around his fingers as he turned her over roughly onto her hands and knees. He yanked at her jodhpurs, pulling them down to her knees as she pushed desperately against the material, trying to open her legs wider, fighting against the restriction but only managing to part her legs a few inches. But he ignored it, straddling her legs with his own and forcing his way into her tight pussy, sinking deeply inside her with one hard thrust.

His hands squeezed her waist; strong thighs pushed hers closer together so that her pussy gripped him even tighter. Her arms gave way, her hands spreading out at her sides, clutching at the straw as she matched his rhythm. Then she couldn't think of anything else, could only feel the sensation as he pounded into her. Her

3333333333

greedy pussy closed even tighter around him, squeezing, wanting, until she hadn't any control left and she had to let the waves of her orgasm roll through her body. As they did, he gave one final thrust and grunt of satisfaction and she knew she'd been well and truly fucked for only the second time in her life.

***

Saul eased his grip on her waist, the imprint of his fingers like a brand on her skin as she sank down onto the soft straw. He waited for his breathing to even out, then ran his fingers through his hair, pushing himself up unsteadily to his feet.

Shit, that wasn't supposed to have happened. He felt out of control, drunk with lust. Last night should never have happened, and now this. And right now all he really wanted was to know that it was going to happen again. And again. Shit.

She rolled over with a soft groan and looked up at him, and despite himself he had to smile. There were bits of straw sticking out from the mass of red curls, and she looked thoroughly shagged out. He picked up the torn G-string, dangling it on one finger. "Normal riding wear?"

"I like to feel unrestricted when I'm riding."

"Oh yeah, I gathered that, Lady Godiva." He dropped the grin. "Was that a good idea?"

"It was good"—her voice was husky—"but not a good idea." She ran her tongue over her full lips and he felt his cock stir again in response.

"Was that part of the plan too, then?" It was a quiet, sexy drawl, but he could hear a note of doubt in it, an uncertainty that made him feel a complete bastard. Even though, since he'd realized who she was, every part of the plan seemed to have gone flying out of the window. The fact that she thought he operated like that left a sour taste in his mouth; the fact that he knew people who did made him wonder for the first time if he was in the right game.

"Hey, don't look at me like that. It was you who started the wet T-shirt competition." She gave a self-conscious grin. "But no, that wasn't part of any plan; do you really think I'm that kind of a man?"

"No, maybe not." She shrugged, sat up, and pulled her bra back over the gentle curve of her breasts. "Not really." A soft sigh escaped, and she frowned as though she was straightening everything out in her head. "Just checking. I don't usually act like this, so I don't know the rules."

"If it's any help I don't usually act like this either, and as far as I know there aren't any rules." He spoke softly and offered his hand, her small one nestling briefly in his as he hauled her to her feet. And he wasn't sure he wanted to let go of it.

———

"You did know your husband had run up debts?"

Roisin cradled the warm coffee cup and looked at the man opposite, who didn't look at all like a stranger; he looked comfortable, like he owned the place, which it was beginning to look as if he did. "I knew Toby was piling up the debts, yes, but I didn't know how bad it was until he died. He told me he was sorting it. I never knew it was too late, that he'd already defaulted."

"Ah."

"Don't say 'ah' like that, as though it makes any kind of sense."

He ignored the interruption. "And you didn't know he'd put

up this place as collateral?" He took a sip and put his mug down. "You don't remember signing anything?"

"Look, this place is my home—it's my job, everything, the one thing I've got left. I'll pay you back or whatever; there must be some way I can…" He met her gaze, but she could tell if he'd been anyone else he'd be looking the other way. It was either worse than she could possibly imagine, or he just wanted this place to sell on. To make money, more money than she could offer him.

"If you can raise the money, then fine, I'll sell to you."

Oh yeah, the words "hope in hell" sprang to mind. "At a profit?" Why was she even asking?

"Just enough to cover my costs. This is just a business deal for me, Roisin."

"And that makes it okay, does it? Just business?" She stood up abruptly, the chair legs screeching against the hard flags of the kitchen floor. She needed to separate herself from him, from this. It was easier with her back to him, except she was looking out at her riding school, her horses. The things she'd just been told weren't anything to do with her anymore. None of it was, which left her with precisely nothing. She bit down on her lip, the sweet taste of blood seeping into her mouth as she stared out blindly, fighting the tears that burned the back of her eyes.

The soft voice hit her harder than anger would have done. "No, it doesn't make it right, but it isn't just my money and I don't see how I can help you."

―――

If there was one thing Saul wanted to do right now it was go over and say the right thing. Not sit here like some dork staring at her slim back, the tense shoulders; not shut himself off and watch her fight her internal battles on her own. But he didn't know what to do about it; he felt impotent. Totally bloody useless.

His hand closed tighter around the coffee mug until the heat burned painfully against the palm of his hand. He had come here to do a job. To look around the place, decide how to break it up. And then do it. Make money. Do his job. And now some sexy slip of a girl in jodhpurs was appealing to the one part of his anatomy that he usually had control over, except something told him it wasn't just his dick that was reacting. She was tugging at something inside him, making him feel a complete loser. Making him feel like he was breaking the rules, which maybe he was—well, bending not breaking. He'd bided his time, moved in at the right time for the pickings, and he hadn't reckoned on her. On guilt. On feeling like a vulture.

"Let's go through your books." He shouldn't be saying this; he really shouldn't be saying this. "We'll see if there is any way you can salvage enough of this business to offer us a solution we can go with, see if you can afford to rent part of the place or something."

"Offer us a solution?" The flat voice made it worse.

"Okay, me. Deal? Or shall we just get this over and done with now? Your choice."

She turned slowly from the window and looked at him. Emerald eyes meeting him head on, flickering over his features as though she was trying to strip the layers away, which he guessed was slightly disconcerting. He couldn't remember the last time— no, any time—a woman had looked at him like this. Properly. Those eyes were the clearest green he'd ever seen, deep and calm. If it hadn't been for the hint of a tremble in her bottom lip he'd have fallen for it, which he guessed would have made it easier to do what he should be doing. But it was that hint of a doubt in her that was disconcerting. That made him want to forget what he should be doing.

"And if I can't, Saul? If I can't magic up some hidden asset, some income I never knew I had?"

She was searching him for answers and he felt like he should be providing them.

"Then we'll have to deal with that, won't we?" Which he shouldn't have said. "But I can't make any promises." Which made her frown, and the twist of unease in his stomach grow.

"Fine."

God, he hated that word, a kind of pleasant defiance. She finally dropped the inquisitor's stare and gave up on searching his soul—maybe, he reflected, she couldn't find it in the first place—and headed across the kitchen in that graceful, controlled, way she had.

He tried not to smile as she lifted the pile of record books effortlessly from the dresser; she looked such a waif, so delicate, as though one rough move would break her. But she was steel—or, at least, there was a core of it running straight through her. She dropped the books in front of him with a heavy thump, then sat down again.

He'd look at those records with her, listen, and then he'd explain again just how bad it was. Because however bad he felt about the whole thing he couldn't see she had a hope in hell of clambering out of the hole her dead husband had dropped her in. He'd watched holes like that being dug so many times, and no one got out.

He shouldn't have touched her; he wouldn't have if he'd known who she was. And now he should keep his dick in his pants, tell her the truth, and hammer the final nail in the coffin. Probably convincing her for good in the process that all men were bastards, but men like him were the biggest bastards of all.

He'd driven up here expecting to deal with some rich bitch; been prepared for a frosty reception and a dressing-down from some snooty cow who thought he was beneath her. That would have made it easier; not nice, but easier. But he'd found Roisin. Empathy wasn't his bag; he was used to open warfare, which he felt a whole lot more comfortable with.

But these rich, spoiled country girls were always given everything on a plate, weren't they? Even if she was cute, and sending him on some kind of guilt trip he couldn't fathom, even if she was different, at the end of the day she was still one of them. Still born with the silver spoon in her mouth, even if it was about to be smelted down.

"You don't have a rich daddy who can bail you out, have you?" Whoa, if there was a look that could kill she'd just shot it his way. He didn't need to be Einstein to work out he'd just said something very, very wrong indeed.

Chapter 3

"WHAT THE HELL HAS my father got to do with you?" Roisin crossed her arms and glared at him. The type of look she gave the kids when they were running wild around the stable yard; the type of look she used to give Toby when he came in drunk and useless with yet another excuse. It worked. Normally. Always. Well always, apart from now. He just looked at her with those smoldering intent eyes, and leaned back casually in his chair, totally unbothered. Bugger.

"This is my money we're talking about, lady, so I'd say any"— his eyes traveled slowly down her body—"hidden assets you have should be considered." And he was doing that—that thing again. She was glad her top had dried out because her nipples were already tightening under his scrutiny and the last thing she wanted him to know was just how much that lazy look affected her. God, one minute he was explaining what hell looked like and the next he was reminding her of heaven, and she really needed to get a grip.

"Well? I thought all you girls had a rich daddy hidden away somewhere?"

Shit, he was annoying. And turning her on, which made him even more annoying. She tried not to squirm. "Well, this one doesn't." She sounded snippy, she knew she did, but she couldn't help it. The last thing she wanted to talk about was her family and here he was poking around as though he had some divine right. She couldn't afford to get angry, lose control. He was studying her as though he'd found the weak spot and was going to prod her with a stick to see which way she jumped.

"I haven't seen my father for years and that's not going to change. Okay?" Obviously not, judging from the long silence that she felt compelled to fill. "He's dead, okay? And no, before you ask, there is no inheritance, nothing. Dead, gone, kaput, nothing." What was it with the men in her life always managing to leave her with exactly zilch?

"Oh. I'm sorry. I didn't mean to…"

"Pry? Intrude? No, I'm sure you didn't." She was getting huffy and she couldn't help it.

"I am sorry, really. I guess we've ruled that avenue out then." His voice crept around her, soft and sensual, heading straight under her defenses. She blinked, feeling her shoulders drop, feeling the anger suddenly switch off. Maybe he was just trying to help, but her father was a story she really wasn't ready to tell.

"Yes." She shoved her hands under her bum to stop the tremble. "I guess we have. What's next on the list, then?"

"I'm not sure." He suddenly stood up, as though he couldn't bear to sit with her any longer. "We'll look at the books later; let's go have a look around the estate first, shall we?"

Fuck. Saul watched her haul herself into the battered Land Rover and resisted the urge to put his hand on her toned bum and help her in. Those jodhpurs were going to be the death of him, although the way his dick reacted every time she got within ten yards it wouldn't matter if she'd been wearing coveralls and a hockey mask.

He marched around and yanked the other door open. What the hell was he supposed to do now? She was making him feel uncomfortable, like he was some hyena waiting for her to weaken before he went in for the kill. Except it wasn't funny and he wasn't playing. And he didn't want to hurt her. But it was just a frigging farm at the end of the day, a run-down farm with some ponies and a few horse-mad girls coming for riding lessons and not paying enough to cover the cost of the horse nuts and hay, let alone a mortgage. Sitting with her in that shabby kitchen had made him feel everything except businesslike, but coming out here wasn't helping either.

She was giving him a quizzical look. "You still want to look around?"

"Sure." He smiled, trying to release the tension in his jaw. "Try and stop me." His eyes traveled down over her body. "I want to see every single thing."

She gave that small, self-conscious laugh that made his stomach turn deep down. He'd come up with something. Eventually.

"Hit the gas, girl." He looked out of the window; countryside and battered chic wasn't really his thing. The landed gentry definitely weren't his thing. But getting his hands on her again was, even if she was one of them. Out of his league, right out of his stratosphere.

Saul felt the tension ease as she nosed the Land Rover down the steep hill. She was relaxed now, confident; she'd lost the bossy edge and she handled the battered vehicle with a familiarity that said she'd probably been driving cross-country since she could reach the pedals.

"That wood"—she pointed to the trees on the edge of the field—"is my boundary."

"Any other boundaries I should know about, Roisin?"

The green eyes met his. "Not very subtle, are you? But seeing as you ask…Oh, sure, I have lots, lots of boundaries." Her mass of hair was still tangled from their earlier tumble in the straw, and he could smell the alluring scent of woman that surrounded her. Her smell, her own unique, distinctive blend of want, of need.

"Do you mind if I explore them?"

She had pulled the handbrake on, knocked the gear lever into neutral. As he looked into her eyes, they darkened with an invitation he couldn't ignore. Her lips had parted slightly, lips he could imagine wrapped around his hard cock, lips that held a promise of something more than quick satisfaction.

"I thought you'd already done that." The husky edge set the hair on the back of his neck bristling.

The alabaster skin of her stomach was pale against his tanned hand as he pushed her top up, leaned forward to kiss its soft curves just so he could hear her moan of satisfaction. "I've only just started." Her breast filled his hand perfectly, and she let out a little whimper as his fingers tightened around the hard bud of her nipple. He squeezed harder until her breath quickened and she tipped her head back, exposing the long, slender column of her neck. His eyes narrowed as she ran her damp tongue over the full red lips, circling, caressing her own mouth, and it dragged a groan from him as his balls tightened painfully. The green eyes shot open; and for just a moment she stared unseeing at him, before she reached out, her hand fumbling at his belt, dragging at his zipper impatiently.

The coolness of her long fingers against his hot cock sent a shiver through him that had nothing to do with temperature.

She hesitated, then slid her soft hand down the length of him, slowly leaning forward and dragging another groan from him as she lapped around his rim, her warm, damp tongue flicking at the sensitive underside before circling the top of him, spreading his precome in a long, sensual lick that made his hips jerk forward and his balls tighten.

Soft lips wrapped around him, a warm, firm caress, and he pushed his fingers deeper into her hair, swearing under his breath as his cock threatened to explode. Reciting the alphabet backward might be some people's idea of a distraction, but right now he couldn't think of anything that could help him. Dammit, he just couldn't think. He threw his head back, shut his eyes, tried to distance himself from the sweet torture he wanted to prolong. Her fingers tightened around the base of him as she slid her red lips down his length with a slow stroke that made him want to scream, her hair brushing against his stomach with the lightest of touches that made every nerve-ending cry out for more.

"Oh Roisin." She eased up, her tongue flickering against him until he was almost out of her mouth, and he glanced down. "Don't stop, for God's sake." She flicked a look at him under those long eyelashes, then dipped back down again, slowly taking him into her mouth, her hand twisting as she pulled up again. He groaned and she seemed to take it as a cue, sliding her mouth up and down with slow strokes that grew faster and more confident, her tongue flicking into the sensitive V on every upward stroke, sending a shard of need to his throbbing balls. He fought the urge to thrust into her throat, but he didn't need to thrust; she took him deeper until he could feel her tight throat muscles closing in around his tip, squeezing and then releasing just at the moment he felt he couldn't hold back. Then she was building up the rhythm, the warm dampness of her teasing, until he couldn't hold it any longer. He gripped her head, thrust his hips, and dimly heard the guttural roar that was dragged out of him as he came in uncontrollable, strong bursts that left his stomach trembling.

"Shit."

She was still licking him, licking her lips, as she lifted her head up; she paused to circle the head of his cock one last time before she sat up straight.

"Is that much, you know, come, normal?"

He knew he was grinning like some stupid, gawky teenager but he couldn't help it. He tried to keep a grave face. "I really wouldn't know. I've never sucked a cock in my life."

"Oh." She colored, skin flushing bright red almost before he'd finished talking, but she grinned back. "Are you going to put it away, then? 'Cause some of us have to go shoveling shit."

"Eh?" He blinked, trying to clear his head.

"Muck out the stables."

"Ah." He zipped up his trousers. "Do you never bother tidying away after giving head?"

She stuck out her tongue as he straightened himself. "I'd hate to have an accident with the zipper."

"Ouch. Well, anyway, you've just given me an idea of how we can save this place. Want to hear it?"

"Normally I'd say yes, but if a blow job gives you ideas, I'm worried."

"Trust me, it could work." He watched her shove the 4x4 decisively into gear and wondered what it would be like making out as the vehicle bounced its way over the rutted field, him in the driving seat, her astride him in his lap. Later, next time. There had to be a next time. Which meant she had to at least consider his idea.

—✺—

Roisin stared at him, which seemed to be something she was doing a lot these days, then shifted her eyes back to the windshield as they hit a big rut and the steering wheel nearly yanked her arms out of their sockets.

Trust me, he says, and then he suggests she let him use half the place to run an altogether different type of riding school.

"You want to what?" She couldn't have heard right; her hands tightened on the steering wheel.

"Run a sex counseling place here. Hey, even without looking at your books I know you can't afford to rent the lot and you can't afford to buy it back, right? So we share the place. You pay rent for your bit and they pay rent for theirs, and we see how it goes. I've been struggling to find premises for them and it just hit me how perfect this place is. It's private, tucked away, and"—he was grinning, she didn't need to look, could hear it in his voice—"no one can hear the moaning and screaming."

"Saul!"

He leaned around to kiss her, smelling of sex.

She screwed her head away. "Sex. Counseling."

"Yup." She couldn't look at him, but he still sounded too bloody pleased with himself. "I'm involved with this company…"

"Involved? Funny type of company to be involved in, like they're friends?"

"No, like they're clients." He ran a finger down the side of her face, along her jawbone, setting off goose bumps.

"Clients?"

She ignored his sharp expulsion of air. "It's a business interest. Look, are you prepared to listen or not?"

She shrugged. "Not" would probably be the safest answer.

"I'd make more money just selling off this place, but for some mad reason I'm trying to help and I'm willing to bet this could work."

"It doesn't mean you get another blow job." Why did any kind of sex with him put her brain into happy camper mode and distract her from the real issue: impending homelessness? He was harrumphing: sex, it seemed, was an on-off switch for him. "Okay, okay, carry on." Although she'd really rather he didn't.

"These clients of mine, they've got a good client list but nowhere to go. And you've lots of space you don't need. It would be perfect to combine the two; you can carry on with your horses if you want, and we can run this business alongside. These guys are more than capable of dealing with all the day-to-day running; they just don't have premises or money, and I reckon in the right place they can get back to turning a good profit."

"Combine the two? Alongside? Alongside?" She was getting screechy; she mustn't get screechy. "Are you mad? I've got kids coming here, and middle-aged moms who want to learn how to ride horses, not, not..."

"To learn how to ride their husbands?"

She tried to ignore him, tried not to let visions of naked bodies filter into her head. "And what do you mean, *we*? We, since when has this been we? And if it's such a good business, how come they had to get you involved?" She frowned as she pulled into the yard and switched off the engine. He was making it up, kidding her; he had to be.

"They were being screwed renting premises, then one of the partners bailed on us with some cash." He paused and his eyes met hers, but he was seeing through her; she could almost see the cogs whirring. "Which just about finished them off. But sex sells, Roisin, believe me. And these guys know what they're doing, but they're happy for someone else to take the financial responsibility. I bet they get more takers for their riding lessons than you do for yours."

She scowled. "Smart-ass." Tried to ignore the dirty grin on his face. A grin that was dangerous. A grin that told her he was getting more into the idea by the second.

"I'm not kidding. People are happy to pay for pleasure, real pleasure." His voice deepened back to that liquid chocolate point.

She tried to ignore the warmth swirling in the pit of her stomach. He was mad. What type of girl ran a place like that? "A brothel? That's your solution, that I turn this place into a brothel?"

"It's not a brothel and it won't be you running it. They are trained counselors with clients who pay for therapy, couples who want to improve their sex lives, not just pay for a quick and dirty shag." He smiled. "And as for the 'us' bit"—he leaned in closer until his breath warmed her neck, sending a new tingle down her spine—"we're in this together. I'll let you stay and run your stables, but I want something in return. I want you to act as manager for me and oversee the other side of the riding school, which means you pay even less for your rent. We'll try it for six months, then if you think you can remortgage I'll listen, or I'll let you know if I've decided it's not working and I need to sell." He moved back, and she let go the breath she'd been holding.

"Gee, ta, that's so generous." But she supposed it was generous, and a stay of execution for six months.

He put out a firm hand then, and she flinched as he took her chin and forced her to look into his eyes. "Have you got some other solution?"

"Why? Why are you doing this? What's in it for you?"

She could swear he clenched his jaw. "Call it a gesture of goodwill, belief in you." He paused, shrugged, and she could have imagined his tension. "I still make a profit, I can't lose. Anyhow, it's your choice, but that's my offer." His hand settled on her knee; a warm, firm hand that sent a tingle straight between her thighs to a pussy already throbbing with frustration again. Swallowing his come, feeling that rock-hard cock twitch in her throat, had turned her on more than she could have imagined, and for a moment she'd wanted to just clamber over the gear lever and settle astride him on the seat. She blinked hard to get rid of the image.

"I don't want to shut you down, but I'm not going to sit by and do nothing." The warmth drifted higher. "Every day you think about it is costing me money. I can leave now, be out of your hair within an hour, and you can have a month to move out." He leaned forward and kissed her neck, his teeth nibbling a path of want that made her juices flow. "Or you can go into business with me." He sucked at her soft skin and she clenched her fingers, trying to stop the moan that struggled to escape. "The sex business."

She did her best to ignore him, did her best to ignore the distracting sensations that were tingling their way through every inch of her. She could move away, but she didn't want to. And she didn't really want him out of her hair. Even though it would be the clever thing to do, to just let him go, let it all go.

"I need to keep this place." Her voice trembled as his breath heated up her skin. She had to keep the last thing she had. She'd relied on other people for too long and now she needed to take charge. She dropped her hand on top of his, stopping his steady progress up her inner thigh. "Show me more, and then I'll decide what I want to do."

He moved back then, and the cold air hit her skin where his mouth had been. "Good girl." The smile was warm, but his eyes were burning into her like hot coals, making every muscle in her stomach clench with need. "We'll go video conference them, then you'll decide?"

"Yup." She swung her legs out of the confines of the Land Rover, away from him. She'd look, listen, and then decide. Except she had a horrible feeling the decision had already been made for her, but however dangerous the sex business was, it couldn't be anything like as dangerous as the man who was uncurling his six-foot frame out of her vehicle. And if she did this it had to be alone. No "us."

"I'll help you with that shit shoveling first, then."

"Dressed like that?" Roisin grinned. "It's not the kind of stain that comes out of a designer suit too well."

"Ha, funny. Give me two minutes and I'll be changed into my jeans."

"Designer jeans?"

"Naturally." He gave her a toe-curling grin. "Don't go away."

———

She wasn't about to go away, but she was torn between wishing she had and wishing she hadn't as she watched him muck the stables out effortlessly. A thin sheen of sweat coated his nut-brown torso, a trickle running down across his well-defined abs, giving her a sudden urge to move forward and taste the salt of the droplets, the musk of his skin.

"You don't look like you shuffle paper all day." The words slipped out before she realized.

"Who said that's what I do?" He grinned, straightening and running strong fingers through hair that had curled with the damp.

"But I thought you…"

"Worked in the City pencil pushing, robbing the rich to make myself even richer?" He chuckled dryly, didn't seem offended. "I was a bricklayer when I left school, and I guess the habit never left me; being physical still keeps me sane." The curl of his mouth was wicked, making her breasts feel heavy, aching for his touch. "Don't you find the same? That there's nothing like a good workout?"

He winked, then lifted the pitchfork again, his muscles tensing and flexing under his skin with each swing. Roisin gave up the pretense of work, stopped trying to drag her gaze away from the jut of hip bones she could just see over his low-slung jeans, the worn denim hugging his hips and the muscled thighs, and just stood and admired the view.

Just who the hell was he? That was the bit that really sent a wave of unease through her. For a moment, she considered turning tail and running before she gave in to the urge to jump him. Mucking out would never be the same again. Nothing would ever be the same again.

***

Roisin stared at the laptop screen and tried to ignore the hunk of masculinity at her side, which was tricky when he'd pulled her between his thighs and was breathing down her neck. Very tricky.

The heat of his chest was pressed against her back, the smell of raw male teasing her senses, his cock nudging her bum. She wriggled self-consciously, then froze as he groaned in her ear.

"Not a good idea, trust me."

Nor was sitting on the knee of a seminaked sex god, nor was video conferencing sexperts, if that was what you called them. Even if they did appear to be reassuringly normal. Even if they were enthusiastic and everything seemed above board. Even if it was the only way he was offering out of the mess.

"They can come and look around next week and I'll decide then."

"Nope, tomorrow."

"Sorry?"

"Tomorrow. They'll come tomorrow and tell me if they think the place would work for them, and you can tell me if you want to give it a go or move on. Then we'll sign the paperwork. One way or another." He stretched around her, pressing his body even closer as he typed in the web address of the business. "This is the website and these"—he scribbled on a business card and pushed it into her hand—"are the admin login details." His arm brushed her breast, making her skin tingle, as he ran his finger down the side of the screen. "Once you're logged in you can see these training videos, sessions they've run. Have a look at what they do."

"Saul, why rush? Can't I have a bit of time to think?"

"Why wait? You're either up for it or you aren't, Roisin. I'm sorry about this whole thing, but I gave your husband several months' leeway and he still defaulted on his last few months' rent, even on this very generous agreement. I've got to drive down to the office to sort some urgent business out and then I'll be back tomorrow with Dan and Marie. And you can decide." His tone was soft, but there was something about it that made her look, meet his gaze. It was almost like he was daring her, throwing her a challenge he didn't expect her to rise to. Almost like he was doing it to make himself feel better, offering a way out that he knew she couldn't, wouldn't take.

He stood up, broke the contact, and kissed her on the nose. "I'll let myself out, leave you to do some research. Up to you; you can take it or leave it, your choice."

———

Roisin stared at the screen. Dan and Marie, the sexperts. She bit the inside of her cheek. She felt like she was being bullied into something, cornered, but she didn't quite get it. He'd thrown down the gauntlet; she'd seen it in his eyes. But why? Why make an offer he didn't want her to take up? It was almost like he had to, he felt compelled to throw a lifeline, but if she didn't grab it quick then he was going to reel it in before she could change her mind.

Which made her want to go for it. Despite a niggling at the back of her mind saying that she shouldn't trust him. What was it her dad had said? That old mantra about these brash young City types spelling bad news in capital letters; all go-getters who trample everyone underfoot, money merchants who bleed you dry and ruin your family as they crawl up the slippery slope to the top, not caring who they destroy on the way. Men who just want to make money. Louts who want to change the world to suit them. Oh, she'd heard it so many times, in so many ways. But he'd been proved right; they'd as good as loaded the gun and pointed it at his head. And if she did this she'd be going to bed with the enemy. Not that she hadn't already. Her choice.

—⁓—

Her eyes drifted reluctantly down the list of video titles; she couldn't help it, couldn't stop herself. *Fingers and Tongues, Dirty Talk, Hands On, What He/She Really Wants, Spanking (Starter), Ménage, Bondage (Lesson Two), Masturbation, Toys (Part One), Rough Play*…She didn't want to look, didn't want to get drawn into playing his game. Why was he giving her this option to stay? Why wasn't he just throwing her out?

She pulled the laptop lid down, snapping it shut decisively. She needed time to think, and he wouldn't give it to her. And he wouldn't give her any other choice. It was this or nothing. And he didn't think she'd take this. Not here in the land of raised eyebrows. A smile teased at her insides. It would certainly give them all something to talk about, change the pitying gossip into something more heated.

She poured a glass of wine; let the cool liquid slide down her throat. She'd have a drink, read a book. Relax. Then decide, in her own time, for her own reasons. She knocked off the kitchen light and glanced back. The power light shone out at her from the front of the laptop. No, she mustn't. She really mustn't get involved in this before she'd decided. What was he doing? Making her an offer she couldn't refuse, or one she couldn't accept? She wasn't sure if even he knew which.

Chapter 4

FACE IT, SHE HAD to admit defeat, and put the bloody book down and stop kidding herself she was reading it. She dropped the thing on the bed; all it was doing was giving her an arm ache. It might as well have been in Russian, or upside down, for all the distraction it was providing. She focused; it wasn't upside down, which was some kind of consolation.

Damn it, and damn Saul bloody Mathews. She had to look at that website. She seemed to have spent most of the last twenty-four hours in a state of arousal, orgasm, or postorgasm exhaustion, and then he'd left her with a library of sex videos to look at. And she felt so bloody horny that she couldn't think straight. Let alone lie still. Maybe it was some kind of new business strategy: shag your enemy until they're too exhausted to think straight and too randy to concentrate. Dammit, she needed a vibrator. A big one, preferably rechargeable.

She groaned. Christ, was it only a day since she had met him? One day that had taken her from wondering how to move on from Toby's betrayal, to being shagged senseless by a man who'd found every erogenous zone she didn't know she possessed. One video had destroyed the illusion that was her marriage and now one hunk of testosterone had trampled roughshod over every other certainty in her life. And suggested she run a sex business. Here. In the middle of a countryside that was more about wearing wellingtons and discussions about baking and crafts than sex and spanking. Shit. Maybe it was just her. Maybe wild sex was going on in every hedgerow in Cheshire and she just hadn't been invited to the party? From what she had seen, Toby had certainly been invited; oh yeah, he'd been at party after bloody party. Although, come to think of it, what the hell had she been doing in the field today? Okay, so she'd eventually received her invitation, or at least gate-crashed the party. And she wasn't ready to leave yet.

Maybe Saul had screwed with her brain as well as her body, but from where she stood there were two options. Option one: bye-bye home, bye-bye riding school, and hello hostel for the homeless. Or option two: admit to losing your marbles.

And anyway, hadn't he said she didn't have to be part of it, she just had to take the money and check everyone was happy? Deliriously, orgasmically happy. Easy. And she could do the one thing he never expected her to. Call his bluff and wipe that self-satisfied smirk right off his sexy face. Or she could let him off the hook. Let him win. Give up. Watch him sell the last bits of her life to the highest bidder and leave her with nothing. Argh! She pulled the sheet up over her head.

Well, screw him. She was sick of letting men have all the fun, men telling her what to do, sick of everyone telling her how she should behave. And sick of wondering what she should do next. And she really had to see what this sex therapy business was all about.

The soft satin of the nightgown caressed her thighs as she padded across the landing, sending a shiver of something straight down to the base of her stomach. Every sound echoed in the kitchen, and it suddenly felt far too large and strangely exposed. She grabbed the laptop and hugged it to her, feeling like a naughty schoolgirl about to have a midnight feast, and decided the intimacy of the study was a far better place to do her exploring.

The soft leather of the swivel chair molded warmly around her body and she ran a finger over suddenly dry lips, capturing the tip between her teeth and flicking her tongue over it, suddenly hesitating as the anticipation curled inside her. For a brief moment she closed her eyes, sucked the tip of her finger. But all she could see was him, Saul. Sucking her fingers, the warmth of his mouth and the flick of his tongue teasing her and sending a need she didn't know she still had coursing through her body. She snapped upright, dropping her hands into her lap. This wasn't about him, this was about her. Her future. So far, her plan for sorting a new life out wasn't going too well; the page was still blank, apart from completing Sam's first task—"have wild monkey sex with the first man you see." Yay, she was a success. Sam would be proud—that was if she ever dared fess up. And Sam, if she was here, wouldn't be hesitating about getting involved with this whole sex therapy business; she would be powering up and pressing "go." But she wasn't Sam. Oh well, just get on with it, girl.

She opened the lid; the laptop sprung into life and her stomach did a flip. All she could hear was her own heartbeat thundering in her ears. She'd have one quick look to see what it was all about; one look so she could check whether Saul was just winding her up, or whether he was dragging her into some weird, kinky world that had more whips and spurs than her own yard did. She ran the mouse up and down the list. *Well, weird and kinky world, here I come.*

"Bend over there, now." Roisin jumped as the low, silky command filled the small room, sending the mouse spinning across the desk. Her pussy clenched in response as the picture flooded the screen, as the girl meekly leaned forward over the padded bench, long, slim legs stretched in a perfect V that led from sinfully high heels up to a smooth, rounded bare bottom, a thin, black thong snaking up between the cheeks.

Her nails curled into the leather arms of the chair as a rush of heat burned across her skin. She bit her lip. The pale buttocks were clenching and releasing in what had to be anticipation, and Roisin's nipples hardened in response, peaking against the satin of her gown. A large hand was squeezing gently, a hand that looked so capable, so inviting, so much like the hand that Saul had touched her with, and she tensed expectantly for the touch, her hips shifting on the chair.

A shiver ran across her skin; she pushed back deeper into the leather as the hand rubbed firmly over the soft mounds of skin and the girl whimpered, sending a zing of want straight between Roisin's hot thighs. She squirmed in the seat, trying to ease the familiar ache that was starting to build.

"Spread your legs wider, now." The voice was softer but firm, almost familiar, with an edge of control that you didn't argue with, the type of voice she remembered from her days at the private all-girls school as that one vicious teacher had instructed the girls to touch their toes, swishing his cane through the air impatiently. A sound that brought back the sense of fear and excitement, encouraged the heady race of hormones.

The girl obediently edged her thighs wider apart, and Roisin felt her own part as a second man edged into camera shot, a man she instantly recognized. Dan, the male half of the therapy business. He put a steadying hand on the girl's back and a visible shiver ran over the body, her buttocks tightening and lifting as she gasped.

"Such a naughty girl." His voice was softer, more sensual than the other man's. He trailed his finger along her spine so she quivered and a soft moan filled the air. The finger came to an abrupt halt when it reached the black lace. Roisin felt a rush of heat to her pussy as the caramel tones ran through her body. "Naughty, naughty girl. So we are just going to have to punish you. You want to be punished, don't you?"

"Yes."

The breathless word made Roisin squirm once more, her breath quickening.

"Yes what?"

"Yes, er, please?" The soft voice had a hint of a tremble in it, and the girl's fingers tightened on the edge of the bench.

He tilted his head slightly and nodded toward the other man, a shadowy figure tantalizingly out of view, with a slow smile. "I think you should spank your naughty wife, don't you?"

The man seemed to hesitate, running his hand over the tense buttocks again, caressing and gently kneading, his fingers pressing to leave small indents in the soft flesh. He slowly lifted his hand, held it in the air only inches away. Roisin's heart pounded in her chest, and her breath caught in her throat as her breathing, their breathing, wrapped around her in the small room.

The sound of a slap suddenly rang out and she took a sharp intake, clamping her thighs together as the girl yelped. The hand lifted, came down again, on the other cheek this time, the sound echoing around her. Roisin's gaze fixed on the red mark left on each pale buttock and her tongue snaked out to dampen suddenly dry lips, her hands reaching up to close around her breasts.

The blows fell steadily, and with each slap Roisin's pussy clenched and she squeezed her tits in time, her fingers tightening around her nipples while the girl cried out in a mixture of pain and need as her bottom gradually changed color to a hot, burning red. She couldn't take her eyes off the hand as it rose and fell; the hand that had been so gentle, so sensuous, now hard and demanding. She tweaked and pulled harder at each growing bud, squeezing and twisting until a thrill of pain shot through her, until her pussy started to pulse. The bottom was glowing, the girl squirming against the leather of the couch she was leaning over. She was panting, her legs had drifted farther apart, exposing a pussy that was glistening damp with her juices as she alternately moaned, and then cried out, writhing and lifting her bottom in anticipation, kicking out her legs.

A damp trickle of juices coated Roisin's thighs as she clenched them together, and she pressed back, rubbing her slit against the soft leather of the chair. The girl was begging, rolling her hips as the next blow fell. She reached down, the satin of the gown slipping apart over her drenched thighs, her swollen labia already parted and ready for her finger as she leaned back in the chair, and it could have been Saul on the video, Saul bending lower, his broad, familiar back to the camera. Roisin gasped as her finger slipped in deeper, her pussy grasping as the man with dark curls swam in front of her sex-blurred vision. Saul. It was Saul. Then he was gone and the girl was squirming and she could have imagined it. It couldn't be Saul; it was just her mind wanting him, imagining him. Imagining the man who'd had her writhing beneath him in the stable was now spanking the girl's bottom. Her hot, glowing bottom. Spanking her until she cried out, until she squirmed with pain, until her throbbing clit, her swollen pussy were dripping with juices and begging to be touched.

She closed her eyes, hearing the slaps, the moans, as she reached deeper inside her slickness with two fingers. She pushed in a third, opened her thighs wider, sliding down on the chair and lifting her hips as she reached higher inside, curling her hand to caress the spot she knew would make her come. He was spanking the girl; Saul was making her moan and wriggle on the padded bench. She fucked harder with her fingers.

Her pussy was trembling, pulsing, as she thrust her fingers in and out, desperate to fill herself. She ran her other hand down over her stomach, the way the man had rubbed that pale bottom before he'd started spanking it to crimson, the way Saul had stroked every inch of her own pale body.

The contact making her gasp and arch her hips, she rubbed just above her mound, hearing her own sigh. She reached down farther, wanting to find her swollen clit as Saul had, wanting to make herself ache again with the urgency he'd created. Soft gasps in the background broke into her mind as she became dimly aware that the sound of spanking had stopped, replaced by urgent moans, but it didn't matter. She didn't need to see anything, just needed to feel her fingers inside her swollen pussy, to remember how it had felt last night, this morning. She could hear his silky voice urging her on, telling her to come, telling her to let go.

She pressed more firmly against the hot, swollen bud of her clit with one finger, pressing harder and deeper with her other hand, feeling her warm juices dribble down her fingers, onto her wrist. He was urging her on, demanding she give in and come.

Her pussy was clenching at her fingers, and she rocked her hips, clutching at her hand as she flicked her fingers alternately. Then the shudders were coming faster and shock waves of pure pleasure rocketed through her body. Roisin dropped her head back against the chair and arched her back as she cried out, desperate to milk every last pulse from her body.

———

"Wow."

"Shit." She shot upright and whirled around at the soft voice, nearly falling off the chair at the sight of solid muscle just inches away. Saul. "What the fuck are you doing here?"

Heat surged to her face and she dragged at the gown, trying to wrap it back around her with hands that didn't seem to work anymore, and the smell of her arousal swam around her fingers, filling the air. Fuck. She slammed her thighs back together. Yeah, as though that was going to make any difference.

His hand slid over her shoulder, rested warm against her breast. "I couldn't stay away." The break in his voice sent a wave of goose bumps down her body.

"Don't." Her hand caught his to stop his steady rub against her nipple, which was already hard.

But he didn't stop; he caught hold of her hand, her damp hand, and lifted it to his mouth, taking one finger between firm lips and slowly sucking, sending a clutch of need deep into her stomach. Her pussy was trembling; her fingers were never enough. She needed him inside her to finish the job she'd started.

"You smell gorgeous, taste gorgeous." He reached over with his other arm, parting the satin that she'd tried desperately to pull over herself. Ran a finger up the inside of her wet thigh, thighs that parted wider instinctively.

———

Saul could almost feel his throat dry out as he watched her. Shit, he knew he'd told her to watch the videos but he didn't think she would. And he didn't think she'd watch that one. One he'd hated, until now. But the video didn't matter. She did.

He knew he should say something, let her know he was there, just knew he should. But he daren't stop her; eyes shut, her face soft with arousal, and her lips parted with need. It didn't matter really what she was watching. The only thing that mattered was the way she looked, the way she smelled. He just couldn't speak, break the spell, as she twisted her hips, his cock hardening in response as the silky fabric slipped farther apart, revealing more of her damp thighs, more of the softly rounded stomach that he needed to touch. But when she moaned and started to shudder with satisfaction he couldn't stand back any longer; he had to touch her, had to bury himself in that sweet smell that had been playing havoc with his senses, dragging him closer.

"What are you doing here?" Her voice was catching in her throat as he held her fingers in his mouth. He sucked harder, felt his cock stiffen as the musky sweetness hit the back of his throat.

"Shhh." He swiveled the chair around so she was facing him, so he could see her body properly. The swell of her hips was warm against his skin as he pulled her roughly to the front of the chair, the soft squeak of objection making his cock twitch. He took the small hand back in his, pulled down so their entwined hands stroked across her swollen labia together. Held her hand firm as she groaned, so that when he slipped his fingers inside her heat he took one of hers with them, fighting the sound of her gasp as together they pushed inside her slippery pussy. She moaned as he curled his two fingers up so it was her own finger that was pressing against an engorged G-spot. Her whole body started to tremble and he couldn't stand it any longer; he pulled at his fly with his spare hand, his gaze never leaving her sex-drugged face. His hard cock was in his hand, the drop of glistening precome spreading as he ran his thumb over the head. She was watching him, licking her lips, her fingers still playing with her pussy. He groaned, slipped his feet under the chair, and then yanked her off it and straight into his lap, lowering her onto his stiff dick, which felt like it would burst at the seams if he didn't let that sweet cunt milk him right here and now. His whole cock wasn't even inside her and she was exploding, her pussy grasping greedily at him, her whole body pulsating as she rocked and rode out the orgasm.

"Fuck." He hadn't expected her to come again that quickly; he grasped her hips tight and bucked his own upward as the last bit of self-control abandoned his body. "Fuck, sorry." His voice dropped and he pulled her down to lie on his chest, the soft feathering of her hair against his chest dragging out a last shudder from his body. "I usually have more control than that."

—⌇—

"Have you come back to keep an eye on me?" She heard the muffled echo of her voice against his chest, but didn't want to move. Well, she didn't think she could move. Watching the video had brought her to a shuddering orgasm that would normally send her straight to sleep, but having a follow-up of Saul's cock buried inside her had left her legs more than trembling. She'd never quite understood why sports people were supposed to lay off sex the day before a big event; it had never seemed that tiring. Until now. Getting up the stairs to bed seemed a big event now. More accurately, getting up off him seemed a big event. She'd get up soon. In a bit. She felt his softening cock curl up inside her; her pussy fluttered in response, she shut her eyes tighter, concentrating on the sensation, knowing it could make her come again. He groaned as her body pulsed softly around him. The last of the feeling ebbed away and she took a deep, steadying breath. He'd come back, and she wanted, needed to know why. "You did, didn't you?" Shit, she should thump him, or something, or nothing right now because she really didn't have the energy.

"Not exactly to keep an eye on you."

"Liar." She snuggled deeper against him, the rough hair on his chest coarse against her tender nipples, and he groaned. So she tried it again.

"Stop it, Miss Sweet and Innocent. I managed to sort out everything I needed to on the phone so I thought I might as well just head back and…"

"Help me make up my mind?"

"And answer any questions you might have before Dan and Marie turn up. So"—he shifted himself into a sitting position and pulled her with him, onto his knee—"you like a bit of spanking, do you?"

"I didn't know people—well, people actually did that for real. Are you sure they do?" She swallowed, a flood of warmth curdling in her stomach. It could have been because of the heat of his hand through the thin satin wrap, or it could have been the heat of his thigh against hers, or it could have been the image of that pink bottom that had just leaped into her mind. And wouldn't go away. He laughed, and her stomach twisted in a new direction.

"Oh, people do it all right, and lots of other things." His fingers tightened slightly around her waist and she could feel her nipples hardening in response. He leaned forward, snaking a hot tongue over the thin material. Oh God, why hadn't she gotten thick flannel pajamas like any self-respecting country girl should have? "What made you pick that video, then?" His warm breath was against her ear sending a shiver of something straight to her pussy.

"I er—I didn't. I just closed my eyes and clicked."

———

Saul smiled inwardly and buried his face into the sweet-smelling mass of hair, feeling her body tighten almost imperceptibly. He'd reacted like some out of control idiot when he found her with her fingers in her pussy, but now the old feeling of panic was hacking away at him as the past peeked above the parapet. He needed a diversion, even if it meant getting her to talk about things he was sure he didn't really want to hear, things that were none of his business.

"Did you and your—er—husband never play games, then?" That subject should be off-limits, but he couldn't help it.

"Toby was far too polite to do anything like that." She shifted in his arms and he had to lean closer to catch the small voice. "Well, to me anyway. He—um, serviced me, I suppose you'd call it, and then went off somewhere else for his dirty shagging." She paused. "Well, that's what I presume he did."

"Ah, I see." Except he didn't. How could anyone have this woman in their bed and not want to shag her brains out? Every which way. Maybe it was an upper-class thing; not that he understood the upper class, or knew anything about Toby Grant, for that matter. But he hadn't liked the man, whatever. "Are you sure about that?"

"Oh yeah." Her voice whispered soft against his skin. "I saw it."

"Shit, you walked in on him?"

"No, he had his own set of home videos and he was the star."

Hell, he hadn't seen that one coming. And it had sent him right back where he didn't want to go; he could be in real trouble here if he wasn't careful. The panic spun like an unwelcome pinwheel firework in his gut and he pulled her tighter to him, trying to still it. "So you've got a box full of toys to keep you happy, then?"

"Toys? What do you mean, toys?" Her head had shot up, her voice a mix of indignation and shock, and it took all his control not to burst out laughing. He pulled her back down, his silent laugh rolling through his body, stilling the edginess inside him.

"I thought vibrators were every girl's best friend."

"Oh yeah, sure." She fidgeted, which meant she'd probably at least thought about it.

"No, I mean it. I blame men like Toby." She stiffened in his arms and he stroked a hand through the thick curls, stopping to tighten one around his finger. He leaned in closer, liking the smell of her hair, letting his lips brush against it and stir up the exotic floral mix. Just wanting to talk, about anything and everything, just to keep her there. "Did you know that back in Victorian times women who weren't getting shagged senseless by their uptight hubbies used to be sent to the doctor to be massaged to get rid of their hysteria? And you know what that meant, don't you? They were queuing up to be finger-fucked—" He pulled her closer against his hardening cock. Shit, was this really the diversion he wanted? "But those poor doctors got shagged out, servicing all these desperate housewives." He could feel his cock already twitching against her thigh.

"Don't be ridiculous." The nervous laugh clutched at him just where he didn't want it to.

"It's true, so the doctors installed vibrators in their consulting rooms." He cupped his hand around her bum, reaching farther to curl his fingers until they pressed against her slit, damp warmness seeping through the silky material.

"You're making it up." Her voice had a quaver in it as she pushed down against his probing fingers.

"No, I'm not, those poor doctors had to play with pussy after pussy, making them all warm and wet and quivering like yours." As he spoke, he probed deeper. "Then people got electricity in their homes, and you could spend your money on a kettle or a vibrator. Some choice, eh?" He pushed her hair aside; let his lips glide down the soft skin of her neck, before nipping it gently with his teeth. "After all, if the doctor ordered it, then it must be good." She whimpered as he reached the dip where her neck met her shoulder. He sucked, pushing his fingers harder, so the soft material was forced against her lips, forced inside. "Orgasm on prescription." She groaned, squirming against his hand as his tongue circled the fragrant softness of her neck.

She was right; he'd come back to keep an eye on her, he'd

come back because he couldn't stand the feeling of driving in the opposite direction, and risking letting her escape. She moaned, reaching down between her thighs. He'd come back because he wanted to feel that silky-soft skin against his. And he'd come back because he knew he had to explain to her that however much she made his balls ache, however much he wanted to feel her body molded against his, this was business. He had to prove to his father that he could cut it, had to prove that he wouldn't make the same mistakes his dad had made. Let a woman all but destroy him. A woman with a rich daddy.

He really had come back to explain. He suddenly stopped and then, in one motion, flipped her over onto her back on the cold, hard floor. Her lips were parted, her cheeks flushed with need, and those dark eyes were heavy with promise. A promise he wanted to bury himself in. She was looking up at him with those deep green eyes, waiting. He could stop all this now. He could stand up and walk. Give her six months to start turning enough of a profit to satisfy him. Walk and never see her again. He sank lower, held himself on his forearms just above her as she lay waiting for him. She parted her thighs, reached up with her legs, the warmth of her calves against his waist. The muscles tightened in his arms as he slowly lowered himself, as she pulled him firmly down. Her warm breath reached up to him, drawing him closer. Her legs wrapped around his waist as she lifted her hips to meet him; as his mouth crushed hers, she melted, soft underneath him, her lips parting wider, inviting him to explore. The second he pushed his tongue deeper she took it, sucking, sucking as though it was his cock.

He closed his eyes as he tasted the sweetness of her mouth, a sweetness he couldn't walk away from. She was drawing him in deeper, sucking harder, rolling his tongue in her mouth; with a growl that he knew had to be his, he sank down and let his cock slide deep inside her warmth, all the way until his throbbing balls were hard against the soft welcome of her damp pussy.

Chapter 5

SAUL WATCHED AS SHE stirred the cup of coffee. His stomach muscles tightened; he didn't want a neat picture of domesticity. That was old news, along with that damned video he'd caught her watching. He had to sort business today, had to put things back on the right footing. And then he'd keep away. Before the past came crashing back into his life. He didn't want her being turned on by the sight of him spanking his ex, the woman he'd thought he loved, the woman who'd taken and taken from him until there was nothing left to give even if he'd wanted to. He felt the pulse in his jaw. Maybe Roisin was just the same after all; maybe the way she'd been turned on by that video was just the start. Maybe he should be taking the easy route, just putting her off this whole thing and walking away. But it mattered that he put this offer on the table, that he gave her a choice. Then at least he'd have done the right thing for once in his life.

"Hey." She was grinning a wary welcome. Maybe not. Maybe he was being daft, but he wasn't going down that road again, whatever the temptations. All he had to do was get the papers signed, one way or another, and then stay away.

"Hey yourself." He watched as she poured a cup for him, as the steaming water hit the bottom of the cup and he waited for the waft of coffee to reach him. Instead, the waft of something fresh and sweet came straight from her body and hit him in the gut. His eyes fixed on the delicate hand, trying to block out his other senses. Fingers that were trembling slightly, that held the spoon just that bit too tightly. He glanced up and his gaze met the soft green eyes, darkened like moss. He'd keep his distance later, once she was okay, once she knew what she was doing. "Hey, come here."

She needed coffee. A rush of caffeine to give her a boost and make everything normal. She slowly swirled the spoon around, not wanting to let go of something familiar, and studied her fingers. Every bit of her was shaking inside, but at least it was hardly showing in her hands. The initial shock of learning her home was no longer her own had worn off; she'd known deep down that it was coming, she just didn't expect to hear anyone say it out loud. She'd thought she still had some control over the situation, the timing, thought she had months of talking to solicitors and passing letters back and forth. She'd never thought for one moment that it was already too late to do anything about it.

Seeing Toby in all his naked splendor, shagging that pneumatic blond, had shocked her more. But now she had to decide, pick a path. And this time it was going to be her decision.

His warm hands hit her waist, making her feel squishy inside; his warm lips on her neck made her feel something different altogether. She wriggled free and took a step backward. Distance was what she needed. Distance from temptation.

"You'll be fine, honest." The seductive drawl made a promise he probably couldn't keep.

"From where you're standing, yeah."

"The business will be fine, you'll be fine." He was shrugging as though she was a moron, as though it was all straightforward. "I'll sort it."

"I don't want you to sort it." She really didn't. She was sorting this herself, picking her way. Making it work. And if it didn't work? Well, she'd know exactly who to blame. She put the cup down, misjudged, and it hit the work surface hard, sending a splash of coffee.

"Well, tough shit, darling, because I'm involved, we're both involved."

"Huh. We'll see. And I'm only involved if I decide to do it." If. That was the problem, though; she didn't want any "we." She wanted that one-night stand to have been a one-night stand. And the only way she was going to be able to consign it to honorable history was if she could keep as many miles as possible between them.

"So you've changed your mind? You're going to give up and go, just like that?"

She looked into the eyes that suddenly seemed darker, more controlling. "I didn't say that. I haven't made up my mind yet, so I can't change it, can I?"

"Fine."

"I'm not going to let anyone bully me into this if I feel it's wrong for me. I'll find something else." Somehow. Shit, what if she couldn't?

"Sure." He picked up the spoon she'd discarded and jabbed it into the sugar bowl.

"You don't take sugar." She raised an eyebrow.

"I suddenly have a craving for something sweet."

"I can't let anyone make up my mind for me, Saul, not even you." The spoon clattered into the sink. "Shagging me senseless last night doesn't change anything, this is my decision." A muscle was twitching in his jaw; she was making him mad. But she couldn't stop pushing; he had to know that if she did this it was on her terms. Alone.

"I'm not out to bully you, Roisin." The tight, low voice had a warning tone. "I just thought this was a reasonable solution."

"What, a solution that suits me or just you?"

"That suits everyone. This is about business, pure and simple; it isn't about shagging you senseless. How many times do I have to fricking say that?"

"Until you stop fricking doing it." Why the hell didn't he get that? The fact that every time they did it, it made the whole thing harder, more complicated. "Why've you been shagging me at every opportunity, eh? Hunting me down before you came here? Coming back last night to soften me up?" She pulled farther away from him. Maybe she wasn't being fair. But life wasn't being bloody fair. She wasn't sure she wanted to just stop this fling yet, and she didn't want to walk away from a place she'd fought for unless she had to. This place meant more to her than he could ever imagine, she'd had more battles, more heartache to keep this place than in the rest of her life put together. But was it worth prolonging the agony? It would take more than divine intervention for her to be able to buy it back.

"I didn't hunt you down and you know it. That was something that just happened and we both bloody wanted it, so don't pretend you didn't. I didn't need to soften you up, Roisin, I didn't need to do anything. I just wanted you." He sat down and looked. And he looked like he was being honest, or a bloody good actor. "Admit it, Roisin, you wanted it too."

"Okay, I admit it, I wanted it." She shrugged. What was not to like when someone attacked you with animal lust?

"I'm not forcing you into doing this. I just don't want to take everything away from you if there's no need."

"I need this place."

"I know. Don't worry."

"Sorry, but that's easy for you to say. I do worry." He was making it hard to distrust him, making it hard to push him away.

"Roisin." He'd moved closer, into her personal space, a space he seemed to occupy as comfortably as if it was his own. "I'm not trying to push you either way but"—he flicked her hair back over her shoulder, the nearest he got to contact, but enough to send a tremor through her body—"you enjoyed that video, didn't you? It didn't disgust you; it turned you on. You like sex, love it, so why not help other people enjoy it more. Where's the problem?"

You, you're the problem. "Wow, big surprise, I like sex. It doesn't mean to say that I want a new career in it. Look, I'm not stupid. You're offering me a way of staying, so I'll consider it, but if I don't think it's for me then I'm walking." *Though where the hell to I don't know.*

"Is it about what other people think? You don't strike me like the type of girl to be bothered by that."

"Stop trying to manipulate me." She ignored the look he shot at her. "It's not really about other people, though I'm not stupid enough to ignore them. It's you." There, it was out; she'd said it. She paused; she didn't want to be bound to him, to any man, ever again, whether it was business or pleasure. "And the fact that sex just about destroyed everything I ever had, so why should I play the game?"

His eyes bored into her. "Sex—or greed? Sex on its own never destroyed anything."

"And you'd know."

"Oh yes, believe me, I'd know." His lips were tight. "Don't let emotion make business decisions for you."

"I'm sorry, Saul, I'm not you. This isn't just logic, this is about my life."

"What did you mean when you said it was me?"

"I didn't say..." She wasn't going there.

"You did." The sharp rap of the door knocker made them both jump. They stared at each other for a moment.

"Why are you doing this, Saul? Why aren't you just throwing me out?"

"Later."

Which left them both with unanswered questions.

—◁◁◁—

"Hi there, you must be Roisin. We've heard lots about you." The fresh blue eyes and open face hit her like a breath of fresh air, and the bubble of tension that had been building in her head shattered into a million pieces. The instantly recognizable Dan.

"Yes, lots." She shifted her gaze to the dark-haired woman who had one hand outstretched toward her, the other wrapped around Dan. "You've got a great place here; it's absolutely gorgeous, isn't it?"

"It is." She took the hand in hers. "Which is why..."

Dan gave an easy laugh. "Which is why you're a bit wary of turning it into a sex haven?" His grin broadened. "Don't worry. I know exactly where you're coming from, honey."

"I just..."

"Hey, it's cool, you don't need to explain. It's not everyone's cup of tea. When we first started up there were all kinds of rumors about what we were doing, but it's settled down a bit now. Phew, anyone would have thought we were advertising for sex slaves. You've seen the website? Looks almost respectable, don't you think?"

"Yeah, she's had a quick explore." The soft voice breathed into her ear and she jumped. Mmm, *explore*. That was probably just the right word.

"Great, great. Do you mind if we look around before we talk business? We've been in the car far too long. I think I'm going to seize up if I don't stretch my legs. That's unless…?"

"No, sure. I'll give you the guided tour." Smiling was supposed to make you feel better, not give you face ache, right? Okay, she was being a miserable, defensive sod, but the whole thing was a bit surreal. And this was just prolonging the agony. She pulled the door shut and led the way across the garden toward the yard, feeling almost as though she was signing her own death warrant.

"Wow, this is great, look." Marie had clambered onto the fence and sat grinning, pointing out the horses, the fields, as though it was all a dream come true. Roisin let her eyes wander over the familiar landscape, a sight she couldn't help taking for granted, but which had always made her feel good. It wasn't just the color of the grass, the sun glinting off the horses' shining coats, the peaceful buzz of nature uninterrupted by man. It was more than that; it was a kind of all-encompassing vibe of everything being all right. Harmony, she supposed, was the term. And it used to be hers.

A hand that felt almost possessive sneaked around her waist as Saul moved in closer. Something that was too much of a turn-on for comfort. "Poor Marie, she doesn't often see the great outdoors."

His warm voice, the warm hand immediately sent a zing straight to her nipples.

Marie threw a punch in Saul's direction. "Cheeky bugger. It is fab, though, Saul, you were right. It's perfect for us."

Yup, it was fab, great, fan-freaking-tastic. Roisin had always loved it here, but lately she'd forgotten to really notice the beauty of her surroundings. "I love it too, Marie, even if Saul's too much of a heathen to notice. Which is why I'd hate to leave it." Shit, that sounded soppy, and it sounded like her heart was already making the decisions for her.

But Marie's hand was on her arm. "Oh, I'm sure that won't happen. You'll find a way to stay here, hun, with or without us."

Which was nice, but wildly off the mark. It probably meant they didn't know much at all about what was going on. Her life, it seemed, was in the large, capable jaws of the shark that'd crept under her defenses unnoticed, and Dan and Marie were there just in time to watch her being swallowed.

"Hey look at this, Marie. This is the type of place we could use, isn't it?" Dan was standing at the entrance to the outbuildings, buildings she'd once used for lecturing about horse care. Buildings that had gradually been used less and less.

"Er, yes." She snapped out of her mope. She hadn't even thought about what the couple needed; which bits of the stables she'd have, which bits would be theirs. But she knew a man who she was sure had.

"Wow, yeah, this would be brilliant for our chats." Marie had skipped in and they were both standing at the entrance, and Roisin felt a sudden pang. A memory of when she'd first taken this place on. That was once her standing there, all excited with dreams about the future. What the hell had happened to her mojo? The get-up-and-go attitude that could make things happen. If she wanted this place then she could have it, just like they could. It was just a matter of new terms and conditions. All she had to do was ignore her landlord, and ignore what her cobusiness traded in. Simple.

Saul strode in, a hard landlord to ignore. "That's what I thought. And you've got those smaller rooms." He waved a hand casually toward the small canteen, the room she'd set up as an office. How the hell had he taken all this in when he'd only been here briefly?

"People would absolutely love this place. It would be great, wouldn't it, Dan?" Marie bounced her way over to peer in the rooms. "You'd really think about letting us set up here?" Her eyes were almost shining as she moved from one door to the next. As she looked at Saul.

Yeah, Roisin thought, it wasn't even up to her to say yes or no; all she could do was decide whether she wanted to be part of it. She could say no and it wouldn't make a dime of difference, not to them, not to Saul, just to her. He'd do it without her. Or sell it on to someone else to do whatever they wanted with it. For some reason he was throwing her a lifeline, giving her an opt-in that might just mean one day she could buy the place back. For some reason.

She dared a glance in his direction. He was watching her, watching every thought that she was sure was running over her face.

"You can say no, Roisin. It is up to you."

Yeah, yeah, yeah.

He took a step closer and she could almost feel her body waver, not knowing whether to flee or move toward him. "It is your decision at the end of the day, but I don't think you should just walk away unless you're sure." Walk away? Since when did she have the chance to walk away? She could say no, say good-bye to the place. Let him destroy it. Or say yes, she'd stay and help, stay as a lodger, a manager until things got straightened out. Until by some miracle she managed to raise the money she needed. It was a no-brainer.

"This place would work great for us." Oh, why had she known Dan would say that? "It would be perfect, Saul, just like you said." They had finally finished exploring and settled down at the kitchen table with Dan's laptop, as he talked her through the ins and outs of their business. "There's not much to tell really, Roisin, apart from what you can see on the website. It's pretty straightforward." Dan flicked back to the home page. "This is a typical program that people start off with, though we tailor everything, since no two people want the same thing. It's not something you can generalize about, but we have these courses as a starting point. But you wouldn't have to bother about any of this stuff, of course."

She had to ask, she had to. "The—er, videos?"

"Videos?" He looked blank for a moment, then his face broke into a grin. "Oh yeah, our videos. Well, sometimes people want recordings of their sessions, but they're mainly for staff purposes. We're not in the porno market. They're guidelines, a starting point for a therapy session, to discover what people might want and let them see how far we're prepared to go. You know? We've got to be careful to have boundaries, to know what's helping and what is… Well, getting too involved."

Dan took his hands from the keyboard and swung around to look at her properly. "We don't do really kinky, heavy stuff; we're about improving things for people, not pushing boundaries. If people want real pain then they're in the wrong place. We're more about new ideas, a bit of experimentation and working out what you want. Saul will tell you all about that, won't you, mate?"

They both glanced up at Saul, who'd been a barrier behind her, almost as though he wanted to make sure she'd stay the distance, hear the full explanation. His grip on her shoulders seemed to tighten briefly, but she told herself she must have imagined it.

"I've mentioned it." He shrugged. "But I think she needs to hear it all from you."

"Great." Dan went back to the website. For a moment, Roisin looked at Saul's slightly shuttered face before swiveling around again. She hadn't imagined it. For the first time since she'd met him there was something he wasn't Mister Ultra-Confident about.

"We're not hands-on, we don't join in, Roisin. I don't want you thinking it's like one big gang bang."

She fought a smile. Since when did people discuss gang bangs in her kitchen? Her dad and Toby would be horrified, which was quite a good reason to carry on. Or maybe they wouldn't. After all, neither of them seemed to have had a problem finding women who were sex mad. They just didn't want her to be. Maybe she was the one who needed help; maybe she should be signing up for private lessons with Dan and Marie. She should get a damn good discount, anyway.

"We're facilitators, more than anything." Marie's soft, musical voice broke into her thoughts. "We get them to say what they want, because so many people are afraid to talk about it, you know? We can encourage, make them feel it's okay and maybe suggest a few things. I know some people are kind of brought up to be too polite about it; they don't like to say what they want."

Roisin grimaced. Nail on the head.

"But we don't pretend we can help everyone. I mean, there's no miracle cure, but sometimes one session and a good chat can make people realize what they want, make things work out better."

"Or worse." The low growl made them all stare at Saul. "Well, sometimes talking can make people realize they're wasting their breath."

"Yup." Dan laughed. "As Marie said, we're not offering a miracle cure. But do you know how many women haven't had an orgasm with their partner for years and neither of them knows how to sort it?"

Marie was talking almost before Dan had finished. "And don't know about vibrators and all the toys that are out there and the different ways of…"

Tell me about it, thought Robin. She felt like sticking her fingers in her ears, closing her eyes, and humming loudly to block it all out. But she couldn't. Sitting here drinking coffee with strangers and talking about orgasms was just strange, and this was what she was about to sign up for? Except they had a point. And a business.

"Just bring up the figures, Dan, and then Roisin can get a feel for the size of the business." Saul was back behind her, his hands on her shoulders. Hands that instinctively started to massage muscles that had tightened with all this talk of frustration and sexual unhappiness. She fought the sigh that wanted to escape, fought the temptation to lean back and purr like a cat.

"Sure thing." Dan was already bringing up spreadsheets on his laptop. Pointing at client lists, revenue streams, costs, highlighting repeat customers. She didn't have to be an accountant to see it worked, that they had a business with potential.

"But isn't moving out here a problem?" This place was in the sticks; no one drove out here. Which was half her problem; it was the diminishing local trade that had killed her, as people had moved out to get closer to the jobs. The countryside wasn't always a fun place to be.

"Well, it's just that Saul said…"

She took an inward breath. "Saul said." What had Saul said now? His fingers massaged deeper and she braced herself against him, determined to fight the way he was lulling her.

"He just mentioned your B and B business? Said you'd never got it going? Well, residential courses are our big thing; that's what people love, a few days of R and R. They'd jump at the chance to come out here and relax. We were thinking we could offer massages and things like that as well. And the fact it's off the beaten track is a bonus. Most people don't want to run the risk of bumping into their neighbors." Fine, now Dan was offering the prospect of sex-themed staycations. He was looking at her expectantly. Everyone was looking at her expectantly.

"Oh." What else could she say? Even if she did sound half-witted and not at all the kind of person she'd pick to go into business with.

Saul's voice rumbled over her shoulder. "You can't see any problems, then, you'd be happy to go with this?"

Dan shook his head. "No probs. It looks great, doesn't it, Marie? When can we make a start?"

"Give me another hour to run through everything with Roisin

again, and then if she's happy we can set the ball rolling. Otherwise I'm afraid, guys, I will probably be doing a rethink." Fine. So it was all her fault if they lost their opportunity. Fine, just fine. "If it's okay with you I can point you in the direction of a good pub in the village for lunch?" Saul leaned forward slightly so that the warmth of his back was pressed against her. There he was, taking control again. Naturally. First of her body and now, it seemed, of her mind.

If she did this it was both of them. Together. Which meant being stuck with him.

———

"So what do you think, Roisin? It's going to be you who's running the joint because I've other businesses to run."

Ah. So it wasn't a case of them together. Which should have been good, but Roisin felt her stomach lurch again. She was already starting to rely on him, so it was a good job he wouldn't be here. She didn't want him on the premises. Definitely not.

"So come on, what do you think? Ignoring the fact that it's about sex."

"But it *is* about sex. I can't ignore the fact it's about sex."

"It's just a business, a good one."

"Huh, a sound investment?"

"Yes, actually. That's what I deal in, good investments. And anyway, just because you were happy to put up with a shit sex life doesn't mean everyone else wants to."

"Saul." She sat down heavily, farther away from him.

"Sorry, I shouldn't have said that. I didn't mean it."

"No, you shouldn't and, yes, you did."

"But you know what I mean. Look, Roisin, what we got up to was good, wasn't it? Admit it."

"Hmm." She could hate him, she really could.

"Some people are never lucky enough to get that unless they have help."

"Well, aren't I the honored one, then?"

"Roisin, you know exactly what I mean. Sex is a good business to be in."

She did know what he meant, which made it worse.

Saul grimaced. He wasn't really sure he wanted to have this conversation, but he didn't want her to say no. He didn't want her to walk away from this opportunity, from her home. From him. Even if he wasn't sure how long he was capable of sticking around.

"Look, if your—if Toby was still alive, wouldn't you…Well, did you love him?"

"I don't really…"

"You don't have to answer that. Sorry, I shouldn't have asked." He moved closer.

"I do have to answer. I want to. It's just—I suppose I liked him well enough, at first, until…" She twisted her hair in her fingers. "Until he started to go off for sex somewhere else. It was kind of the beginning of the end."

"Come on, you're not going to tell me you were meant to be like a virgin, untouched, untouchable. Mother of his children, perfect wife, and all that outdated crap."

"No, look, you don't understand."

"Try me."

"It wasn't like that. I thought I did love him, and it was fine."

"Fine?"

"Look, he was the first man I'd seriously dated, but he was a bit funny about sex before marriage."

"That's a bit…"

"Shut up. It was fine."

"He wasn't gay?"

"For fuck's sake, I just told you he went off with other women, didn't I? What gay man would do that? We got on fine, but I didn't find out until after we got married about how—well, how involved him and Dad were businesswise and I think he kind of felt, well, obligated."

"He felt obligated?"

"If you're going to keep coming out with crap then I'm not saying any more."

"But how could he feel obligated? Which century was he living in exactly?"

"Finished? Right. Well, he was nice, kind, looked after me and, yes, for your information we had a sex life, and it was fine."

"That word again."

"Oh, fuck off. It was just normal, polite sex that we had when we wanted, and that was all we expected from a marriage. Like most people do."

"Vanilla?"

"Yes, bloody vanilla. Not even a cherry on the top, okay? Which was what I wanted, what most people want."

"No, they don't. I…" It had been on the tip of his tongue to say he didn't. But then his marriage had been far from normal, and far from good. "It wasn't really what you wanted, was it?"

"We were married, Saul." She sighed. "Maybe if we'd, you know, done more before we got married, we might have realized that…"

"He didn't know how to shag you properly?"

"Don't be crude."

"Look, most people don't just accept boring anymore; they go off having affairs when it gets boring, which is why this type of business is popular. Not everyone wants to be unfaithful or have a divorce. They like what they've got; it just needs fine-tuning."

"Wow, what a great analogy. Tune me up before I run off. Look, no amount of therapy would have glued our problems together. Is that what you wanted to hear? Toby felt so bloody guilty in the end about being such a loser. He'd lost all his money, and we were living off mine, in what was really my place even if technically it was his. He was my dad's puppet, marrying me, acting a part, and he felt so fucking inferior that it made him impotent. He couldn't shag me; get that? Not even if his life depended on it. He couldn't stand even trying because he'd just fail again. So off he went buying women, women he could control, a situation he could play God in. No one to judge him, tell him he was a failure. And the more he did it, the more he probably felt guilty. He'd spent his money, then he spent mine on shagging other women. Right? So, yeah, I believe you—sex sells, people pay for the Promised Land—but I'm not sure I believe in it anymore."

"Phewee, I suppose I did ask."

"You did." She started slowly unraveling the twist of hair that had wrapped tighter and tighter around her finger.

"But I still don't get how you could live like that. You like sex, you come alive when you're…" He was starting to sound like some unfeeling bastard again; he forced his voice back down a level.

"What? Shagging like a rabbit? Yeah, I like sex, sex with you if that's what you're fishing for."

He laughed then, he couldn't help it. "I wasn't fishing. It's just you can have lust and love in a marriage. Christ, Roisin, I know you're buried in the countryside, but…"

"Yeah, I know, but no one says it has to be like that." She shrugged. "Look, it doesn't matter." The soft tone brought a lump to his throat. "It was fine. It was easy to live with. Maybe it was just a case of us trying to please other people instead of doing what was right for us."

"It bloody does matter." But who was he to judge? Maybe her solution had been better than his, emotionless, secure. Except she hadn't been any more secure than he had. "You weren't happy, were you?"

"I was okay until I found out about the other women; he was behaving like a complete twat. In fact, he was doing exactly what my dad did. What kind of a relationship is that?" She gave a short bark of a laugh. "Why should he have had all the fun?"

Exactly. "Not the kind for you, or anyone else." He brought his mouth closer to her quavering lips. Ran his tongue over them to still them. He had to. That was all he was doing, until the taste of her need met his. He forced himself to stop, pull back.

"You do know I can't stay here, can't promise you anything." Staying meant answering questions. "I don't want you thinking I'm a complete twat as well."

"Good, I don't want you to, and I'll try not to think you are." Her soft words registered dimly, but his mind was following her hands. Hands that were opening his fly, releasing his throbbing cock; hands that were like soft, cool silk against his heat.

"Roisin."

"Shh."

"Shit." He closed his eyes as her hand glided down his shaft with a firm touch that made his balls ache; balls that she soon cupped with her other hand. She squeezed and he groaned, a groan that seemed to spur her on. A groan that made her drop her head and wrap her lips around him, her warm, wet mouth making him thrust involuntarily. Her throat clutched at the tip of him as she gagged, then he felt her relax, take him deeper into her soft warmth. One firm finger traced along his perineum, sending a rush of blood straight to his already throbbing cock. His fingers tightened in her hair as he thrust into her mouth. This time she was ready; this time she had her throat open and let him pump deeper, let him do the work as she massaged behind his balls, her hand fisting and rolling against him. She was matching his rhythm, letting him thrust deeper into her mouth, letting him hold her head tight against him. "Shit." One last plunge was all he could manage, and all he could think as his fingers pressed deeper into her scalp was that she was his. Then he was coming and she was sucking him, lapping and suckling as she massaged around his aching balls as though all she wanted was every last drop of his come.

He leaned back against the table, slowly straightened himself. She sat back on the chair, her green eyes eating him up. She didn't smile. Just looked at him as though she was working something out. He ran a hand through his hair. Did she really mean "good" when he'd said he couldn't stay?

Chapter 6

"I can't really say no, can I?" It was the perfect business plan, built on a few years' experience with realistic projections. She could see why Saul was convinced that the income from it would be good, and it would give her an extra income of her own on top of what came in from the riding school. It would mean she could stay here, fight another day, and keep the light glowing at the distant end of a long, long tunnel, the light that said one day she might get this place back.

"Well, you can, but I think you'd be a fool. Unless it's too close for comfort and you want to walk away?"

She didn't want to walk away. She didn't want to let what her father and Toby had done destroy her. But signing on the dotted line, signing this deal, bound them together. Her and Saul, for better or worse. And she wasn't sure she wanted to be bound to anyone else ever again. Even if just looking at him made her turn into a meringuey mess inside.

"I run the business?"

"You look after it day to day for me."

For me. Hmm, that said it all, didn't it?

"And I can carry on with my riding school exactly as I do now, no interference?"

He nodded. "That's your business; all I'm bothered about is that you can afford to pay this rent." He pointed at the figures.

"And where's my option to buy the place back? How do I know you'll let me?"

"You don't." He smiled a thin smile. "You'll have to trust me, but I give you my word that, after twelve months, if you can raise the money then I'll sell to you."

"Even if the business is making a fortune?"

"Especially if." He smiled, properly this time. "Dan and Marie are running that business for me, remember. I'll still have the income from it even if you revert to owning the property. And I assume you'll still let us lease the accommodation we need?"

"Maybe." She grinned.

"Ah, I can see I might have to put a clause in place to safeguard my interests."

"You're good at that, aren't you? Safeguarding your interests."

"Very." Which nagged at her mind like it should have worried her. But it didn't.

—⁓—

It was almost as if making a decision had transformed her; there was something within her that hadn't been before, something he wanted to quantify, to remember. But he couldn't quite pinpoint it, couldn't quite pull the elusive fragments together to make sense of.

Maybe it was just confidence, relief. She was spot on, though, he was good at safeguarding his interests, always had been, until he'd fallen for the oldest trick in the book and got involved, got married. But that was in the past. Now he just had to prove to himself, prove to his dad that he wasn't about to lose control again, ever. That this was a sound, logical business decision. Nothing more, nothing less. "Are we going to trust each other, then? They'll be back any minute, so I need to know if you're willing to stay and look after the business for me."

The tumble of curls trembled around her as she slowly nodded. "I'll stay." Then the smallest, sneakiest of smiles broke over her serious features. She had a naughty side, he knew, and it was almost like she'd decided to do more than sign a business deal, as though she'd decided to take a risk and explore the other side of herself.

"You can handle it?"

"I can handle it, and I can handle you…Partner."

"Boss?"

"Don't push it."

"Maybe if you called me sir?"

"In your dreams—or should that be in your wet dreams…Sir."

"I can see I'm going to have trouble with you. Might have to introduce some lessons of my own." He pulled her close, cupping her bum so that she nestled between his hips; so she could feel his cock, which had just discovered it wanted a bit of the action. "And I might have to sort you out before I have to head back down south." He wasn't sure he really wanted to go; he could stay and thrash this out. Literally. Shag her until this stupid obsession for her disappeared. Or he could just fight it, set the rules out now. Which was probably safer, and definitely more sensible.

Roisin could see why Dan and Marie were so successful. The sex industry might not impress her bank manager, but their approach would. Which, sadly, hers didn't.

Saul had efficiently subdivided the property into what she was renting, and what Dan and Marie would use. The groom's flat above one of the stable blocks would be their home. Once, when the stables had been thriving, she'd needed somewhere for her staff to stay, and the flat had been a good investment. But once the money had started to go out faster than it came in, so had the staff. These days, she was the staff. Apart from a teenage girl from the village who helped muck out.

"What about change of use? You can't just run a different business here."

"Sorted." Saul bundled the signed papers away as she cleared away the coffee cups, and felt the swirl of relief tumble uncomfortably with anxiety in her stomach.

"Sorted, just like that?" It had only just occurred to her, but obviously not to him. Which was why she was in a mess and he was in control. Of the home she didn't own anymore, of her life. Everything. For now, just for now, she promised herself. But it didn't make sense: the town council, county council, whoever— they didn't agree to change of use on a property just like that. They were awkward, old-fashioned.

"Well, maybe not quite just like that, but that was one of the things I confirmed with my people yesterday on the phone. I wouldn't have suggested the scheme otherwise."

"But I thought you'd only just thought of it."

"More or less, but it's definitely going through. They'll be moving up in the next day or two, and aiming to start up business within the next few weeks."

"But...You're sure? It takes months."

He laughed. "I'm sure, Roisin. It's my money at risk, remember?"

So that was it. Dan and Marie would be rolling up, discreetly they'd assured her. And Saul—Saul would be disappearing.

Hopefully for a while, long enough for her to get control and forget what wild sex was like, if that was possible with the constant reminder of strangers in the yard in search of sex therapy. What had she just done? How the hell was she going to explain to the villagers what was going on?

"Stop worrying. It's out of your hands now." He reached past her for the bottle of wine.

"But I…"

"Stop, now." He pulled her closer to him. And it was something about his firmness, something about the way he knew just how to hold her, something about his voice. She felt herself stiffen against him. That video—she'd felt stupid thinking it was him. It couldn't be him. But all of a sudden it felt like things she didn't want to think about were falling into place.

"Saul?"

"What?" That hint of command in his voice, the tone she'd never noticed before, but was suddenly recognizable as him.

"That was you; it was you, wasn't it? Why? Why were you there?" Panic started to bubble deep inside her. It had been him, on that video. This wasn't just a business deal for him, something else was going on. And he had a wife. Shit.

"What was me?" She could hear a wary edge in his voice, which said he knew exactly what was coming.

"That video, you were in that video I was watching. What is it about men and filming themselves shagging?" This was Toby all over again, but for some reason it felt worse.

"Yes. Yup, it was me." His voice had a hollow ring now, an abrupt edge he couldn't disguise that made her stomach swirl. "I wondered how long it would take before you realized."

"Well, why didn't you bloody tell me?" The words caught in her throat in a mix of anger and something she didn't want to put a label to. "I was watching you." This couldn't be real.

"It didn't seem important."

"Not important? You've got a fucking wife and it's not important." She was heading toward hysteria at a rate of knots and she bit down on her lip to stop the flow of words. It shouldn't matter to her. It couldn't matter. It wasn't important. He was a one-night stand—with a "too tired to care" clause.

She heard the bottle go down with a heavy clunk. "It was a long time ago. Years ago, another life, and it's got nothing to do with you and now."

"You're married." *I was watching you spank your wife.*

He sighed; his grip on her tightened. "I was married. I'm not now."

"This has been your business all along, hasn't it? It's all about you and your fucking money, and I'm just some idiot who got in the way." His hands burned her arms as she tried to pull free, strong hands that didn't give an inch. She was pressed hard against his body, a body with a warming, heavy musk that she didn't want to like anymore, that she had to get away from.

"No, Roisin, stop it and listen, for God's sake. I wasn't involved; it's just coincidence that I met Dan and Marie again."

"Bollocks, you expect me to believe that?"

"Believe what you want, but I'm telling you. I was just a client when that footage was shot—or rather, she was."

"A client? What do you mean? What kind of client?"

"What the hell kind do you think? We were trying to sort things out between us." His voice rumbled in his chest, resonated through her body as he held her tight against him.

Her jaw tightened, fighting the lump in her throat. "What things?"

"What do you think?" The hairs on the back of her neck rose at his harsh, short laugh.

"But it didn't work?"

"What my ex-wife wanted was far more extreme than anything I've ever had a taste for. That video was just a lukewarm appetizer for her. She wanted a buzz, the thrill of danger, and I couldn't give it to her. Look, do we have to talk about this?"

"You wanted to sort things out?" She closed her eyes. In a strange way, being pinned against him made it easier to just carry on asking things she shouldn't care about.

"Doesn't everyone at first? Until you realize you're just being used."

"You wouldn't just let yourself be used."

He sighed. "I didn't realize what was really happening until afterward. Being involved makes you like that. Stupid." He sounded angry now; his grip had stiffened until his fingers were almost biting into her. "She dragged me along to this therapy session, pretending that she wanted mediation, wanted us to work things out. But it was just her way of introducing me to her world. She wanted pain and punishment; she didn't want love and affection. Everything physical but no mental involvement. She wanted me to hurt her, give her pain, because pain turned her on, made her powerful, and watching me fight it turned her on even more. That kind of stuff is supposed to be about trust and sharing, but oh no, not for Bianca. She was a cow, a stupid, spiteful cow who was never satisfied." Each word stabbed away at something she couldn't imagine. "I should have known by the way she reacted, the way she dived straight in. Dan tried to be diplomatic, but I wasn't listening. He knew she was being destructive, knew she wasn't there to improve things between us. But I just ignored it, until he refused to help anymore."

She felt her body relax slightly against him. "Oh." Fuck, was that all she could come up with? But what was she supposed to say?

"I thought she was everything I ever wanted when she came along, but I was just her bit of rough. Obviously not rough enough, though; when I wasn't prepared to hit her hard enough, she went and found someone who would. That woman tried to destroy me financially, and then she tried to destroy every other bit of me, and believe me, nobody is ever going to do that to me again." She tried to ease her arm from a grip that was now uncomfortable and he suddenly seemed to realize what he'd been doing. He loosened his hold abruptly, rubbed his thumb over the reddened skin. "Sorry." The gruff voice bit at something deep inside. She'd never heard anyone say sorry like that before. His warm lips came down on the spot in a caress that made her shiver. "Sorry, Roisin. It's got nothing to do with you. I shouldn't…"

"I asked."

"You asked, but I still shouldn't…I've never talked to anyone about it, and it's better left that way." He rubbed his warm hand over her arm again with a touch that was firm but so light and sensitive it made her whole body coil up deep inside. "Forget it, I've moved on."

"But you'd be involved in this business again?"

"It's a good business; it works for lots of people. My personal life shouldn't interfere with a business decision."

The anger had completely gone, just like that, and Roisin wondered just what kind of man he was. Maybe it was practice; maybe iron will, because he certainly had that. She should be worried, but she couldn't be right now; she could just feel a strange sensation of something that could have been relief washing through her, and that bothered her more than anything.

"So you know a bit about my wreck of a marriage"—he ran a finger down the side of her neck—"and I know a bit about yours." He traced the same path with his lips. "And now it's time to stop digging and live in the present." Roisin closed her eyes, felt the tingle that ran down, straight to her breasts that already felt heavy with want. He pulled her tighter against him, one hand around her waist; the other cradled her breast, softly squeezing, his thumb running up and down until her nipple peaked into a hard bud of need. "And I know just what you need right here and now." His warm breath against her neck made her squirm back against him as she felt the dampness build between her thighs. He gave a low laugh, his hand moving down to cradle her mound through her skin-tight jodhpurs. "Sexy as they are, I don't think you need these right now, darling." His teeth bit into her delicate skin and she whimpered as he tugged the restrictive clothing down over her thighs, tipping her over the arm of the chair so that her feet came off the floor and he could peel them off completely. She kicked out, struggling to get to her feet, but his hand was on her lower back, a firm, unyielding hand that sent a rush of juices straight to her pussy.

"Oh no, lady, you're just where I want you." He flicked a finger under her black G-string, then traced down, forcing a moan from her as he stroked his finger over her damp, swollen labia and slipped, knuckle-deep, into her slickness. "I love your pussy, you know." He twisted his hand, spiraling his finger deeper, just deep enough to make her push back against him, just enough to make her reach down to massage her clit. But he was quicker, catching her hand and pulling it behind her back. As she wriggled he caught the other one, brought them together, and had her wrists bound with his tie before she could find a way to move.

"You're mine, Roisin," he whispered in her ear and she gasped, suddenly realizing that, tipped up over the arm of the chair with her hands bound, she could hardly move. He ran a finger down her slit again and this time she pulsed in response, feeling her juices coat her pussy, gasping as he opened her lips with a teasing finger and then bent so he could slowly run his tongue up the length of her, pausing to flick at the hard bud of her clit. He stopped, almost as though he was studying her, but with her head pressed to the chair she couldn't move, couldn't twist around to see what he was doing. Something hard and cold was suddenly against her clit, replacing his warm mouth, and her whole body clenched with a mixture of shock and need. "I think riding crops can give pleasure as well as pain, don't you?" It was the metal top of her riding crop, a whip she'd thrown on the table earlier. He eased the rounded top into her pussy, rocking it against her clit and circling it around until it rubbed against her G-spot. She was panting, she could hear it, feel her whole body pulsing expectantly as he pressed harder, slid the tip of the crop farther into her cunt until her body's throbbing made her clench her thighs closer together.

"Oh no, that's naughty." The sharp slap stung, making her body jerk in surprise. "Open your legs." She wanted to squeeze, squeeze the hard metal deep inside her, but he was pushing a knee between hers, opening her up. As he did, he slipped his fingers into her damp pussy, pressing his thumb against her clit, and the orgasm that had been building suddenly surged through her. With the release she opened her thighs wider, willing him on, wanting more. He pounded harder with his fingers, twisting in and out until she was crying out, begging for more, knowing she was grabbing at his hand.

"Greedy girl, aren't you? I'd give you a good spanking, but I don't think you'd care right now."

She tightened her muscles, willing the orgasm that she knew was building again as he increased the speed of his hand. Then, abruptly, he stopped, leaving her gasping. She shut her eyes, squeezing and releasing her muscles, knowing she could make herself come, then she didn't have to try any longer. He forced his cock into her with a hard thrust that sent her forward, straight into an orgasm that shuddered though her whole body, shattering around him. For a second he held still inside her, and just as the orgasm began to fade he started pumping, pounding into her with hard, short thrusts, his hands gripping her hips.

"Fuck me harder."

His fingers were digging into her hips; with each thrust he was slamming her back against him until she knew she was babbling, incoherently begging for him to keep going as her body started to tremble closer to an explosion of heat that built like a furnace inside her. Then she could feel a hot rush of juices as her whole body seemed to open up before clenching in pulsing waves around him, and as she stiffened her legs out to hold him tighter he gave a grunt of satisfaction, and she felt the heat of his come shoot deep into her core.

"Mmm, that was nice." He slipped her hands free, and then bundled her up, pulling her against him and onto the old rug in front of the stove. The strong arm held her, cocooned against his chest. "Maybe I should have put that into the contract somewhere."

"Slipped up, didn't you?" She stretched one leg down so that it slid between his.

"Oh, I'm sure I'll find some way of adding it in. Or I might just spank you until you agree to whatever I want." His voice edged its way through her body, setting off a new tingle between her legs. "It turns you on, that idea, doesn't it?"

She wriggled. It turned her on, and it strayed into territory she wasn't sure she wanted to head for. "The idea does, but"—she bit the inside of her cheek—"I think I'd need to trust someone a lot to go there."

It was almost like he'd withdrawn, even though his body was still wrapped around hers. She felt his stomach tighten.

"And you don't."

She closed her eyes, bit down on her lip. No promises, that's what they'd agreed. So why the hell did he think she should trust him?

Chapter 7

ROISIN PEELED OFF HER damp riding clothes and stepped under the cool jet of water. Not seeing him for two days shouldn't have been a problem. It should have been a bonus. But her whole body seemed to have an emptiness; she was in limbo, waiting.

Dan and Marie had arrived with a small vanload of stuff and she'd kept out of their way, letting them find their feet, but now she was feeling twitchy, and even a hard gallop that had her heart racing hadn't relaxed her. If anything, she was feeling more on edge. There had to be some way of releasing the tension, some way that didn't involve Saul.

The sun was a soothing balm against her back as she strode across the yard, the whole place still and peaceful with all the horses turned out and munching happily on the lush spring grass. It should have been relaxing, but a nervous energy darted around her body as she pushed open the newly erected "them and us" gate that split their business from hers. It swung shut behind her with the slightest of clicks and, for a second, she faltered before turning toward the barn.

A soft murmur of voices carried over the still air; at least they were around, which meant she could get this whole "first day at work" thing over with. And then life could carry on as normal. Well, as normal as it ever would be. She stepped into the shade of the building and the noise reached out again, a soft moan that carried effortlessly on the air. Shit. Her breath caught at the back of her throat. That didn't sound like a breakfast meeting. It sounded like an altogether different type of feast.

She took another step, trying to be quiet. Her foot caught on something and she nearly went flying straight into the building. Shit, double shit. She froze, holding her breath, but no one came rushing out.

There was another moan, a very definite moan that tugged deep down in her stomach, a moan that easily penetrated the wood cladding of the building. She just had to look, there was something going on in there, but if she turned now and they heard her, it would look like she was spying. One quick look, she'd just look and see what was going on, and then she'd decide if she should go in or leave. They couldn't have customers yet, they weren't open; they were probably just chatting.

It came again, a soft, sensual moan of satisfaction that sent a tremor of need straight to her pussy. She edged up closer against the building; the wood was hard against her fingers, scraping roughly against her bare arm. She couldn't just barge in, right into God knew what was going on. She pressed her body closer toward the sound, closing her eyes as the coarse wooden slats rubbed against her cheek, her heart pounding in her chest. There could be no mistaking the sound; it was a moan of pleasure.

Christ, she had to see. Before she let them know she was there, she had to see who was making that noise. And why. She shifted across, under the window, bit down on the softness of her lip as she opened her eyes and edged up so that she could see through the window. And nearly gave the game away.

Fuck. She slid down, her heart doing a crazy dance, and squeezed her eyes shut, but all she could see was them. Doing exactly what she should have expected. Another moan seeped into her consciousness. And she had to see what was happening. She edged back up, knuckles clamped to her mouth because she just knew that if she didn't they'd hear her.

Marie was lying naked across the table, her legs apart and her slick, swollen pussy on view. Roisin stared transfixed at the way the rosy lips squeezed and quivered as though the woman was on the verge of coming, as though she was already coming. She'd never looked at a cunt before, and now she was finding it hard not to. She dragged her gaze away, down the long leg to the large hands that were cradling the slim foot, the red nail varnish stark against the pale skin. Dan. Dan, who was slowly raising the foot higher to his mouth. Roisin gulped as his firm tongue circled the big toe, so slowly, sensually, she could almost feel the touch on her own skin. Marie gave a ragged sigh, threw her head back and started to rock her hips from side to side, mewing with pleasure as he sucked and licked. His mouth left a damp trail as he worked his way down to the arch of her foot and she groaned, trying to pull away, her damp pussy pulsing. He tightened his grip on her ankle to keep her still, sucking and teasing before moving up to her shapely calf.

Roisin felt a shiver of anticipation run through her as Marie's moans got louder. She bit into her knuckles as Marie reached down with a slender hand, stretching out her fingers to stroke her swollen labia, lips that were already parted and waiting. One slender finger dipped into the wet pussy and Roisin swallowed her own moan. The finger curled up, traced along Marie's glistening slit, and started rubbing over her clit in small, delicate circles.

Roisin clutched the window sill, suddenly realizing she was balanced on her toes. Her body swayed in time with the circling finger, the dampness of her own panties pressing against her skin, her nipples prickling as they peaked against the hard, rough wood. She leaned in, pressed her breasts harder against the wall, rubbing her swollen buds from side to side as she squeezed her thighs tighter together.

"Hey." A dark-haired man suddenly stepped forward and she bit back a gasp. He murmured something she couldn't hear and she held her breath, teetering against the building. The man shook his head in admonishment; he took hold of Marie's hand, pulling it firmly away from her pussy, and started to slowly lick the juices from her fingers. Roisin groaned as the heat started to pool more urgently between her own thighs. One by one, he put each finger between his lips, his cheeks hollowing as he sucked, before taking the fleshy base of her thumb into his mouth in a way that made Marie gasp.

Shit, she couldn't take much more of this. Roisin clenched her thigh muscles even tighter together, rubbing; desperate for some friction, some pressure, fighting the sudden urge to reach down and touch herself.

Marie cried out as the man nipped the soft flesh of her thumb between white teeth, and then Roisin almost lost balance as he deftly drew her new friend's two wrists under the table, tying them firmly together with a length of thin rope. Marie squirmed her hips and Roisin mirrored her frustration; she reached a hand down to stroke the ache between her own thighs that she couldn't ignore any longer. She ran her fingers up the inside of her shorts to the crotch of her panties, which was already sodden, and as she stroked along her fabric-covered slit, the sweet smell of her arousal wrapped around her.

She sighed, her finger pressing harder against her dampness as the dark-haired man rubbed against Marie's hip, his large cock obvious under the stretched, worn denim of his jeans. Dan was working his way higher up her leg, nibbling at her inner thigh so that she cried out and bucked her hips. She was begging, and the other man smiled, said something to her, and then, with his eyes still locked onto hers, reached down. Roisin groaned, biting on the back of her hand as he slowly ran his hand down Marie's face, his thumb caressing her lips until she parted them, until her tongue darted out to taste him. He slipped the tip of the thumb between her lips, between her teeth, his features tightening as she sucked, as she tried to lift her head to take more of it into her mouth. With a small shake of his head he trailed the damp digit down her chin, slowly down her neck, his fingers playing gently over the soft skin, making her shudder.

Roisin was mesmerized by the movement of his hand, her own body tingling as if it was her he touched. He made slow, teasing progress down Marie's chest, lazily circling one breast, his lightly trailing fingers spiraling inward until her nipple hardened and grew to a dark peak. Roisin glanced back at his face and saw pure concentration, his eyes slightly narrowed as he repeated the movement on her other breast and then traced his fingers down her stomach so that the muscles clenched and her whole body trembled. His fingers stopped briefly at her navel and he murmured something before carrying on, dancing his fingertips over her naked mound. Then one long finger ran down her damp slit, and she pressed down onto his hand as his thumb started to circle her engorged clit.

Roisin pressed closer, desperate to see what he was doing, wanting to see his fingers dip into the throbbing pussy. She pushed her own sodden panties to one side with a trembling finger, whimpering as she ran the tip over her wet folds, parting them as she opened her thighs. This was what she needed; she gave a soft sigh as she rubbed her clit in time with the dark man's motion, feeling the lips of her pussy swell and part. Closing her eyes for a moment, she let the sensation fill her. The ache spread from her fingers outward and she forced herself to open her eyes, to stop herself from coming too soon. For a moment Dan's blond head blocked her view, then he moved down and started to work his way up Marie's other leg. All the time, the dark haired man was playing with Marie's pussy until it was running with juices, juices that he spread over her thighs. He was teasing her, his fingers dancing on her swollen flesh, never actually slipping inside, and Marie was bucking her hips, desperate for more, desperate for him to probe deeper. Roisin groaned, fluttering her fingers deeper into her own cunt, taking the satisfaction that Marie couldn't. Grinding against her own damp hand.

Dan's mouth had reached Marie's thigh, a thigh that was visibly trembling, and Roisin could almost feel that wet tongue on her own skin, feel his teeth teasing her soft flesh. She was begging for more, bucking and twisting, and still they teased her. She cried out as the dark-haired man moved back up her body to circle her breast, his finger running over the soft roundness in ever-decreasing circles until he was close to her nipple. A nipple that was growing, peaking, until he took it between his fingers, and this time he squeezed and rolled it, twisting and pulling as she writhed under his touch. Roisin forced her clingy top up over her own heavy, swollen boobs, and tugged at a nipple that was already hard. She tweaked harder, pulling it to a higher peak that rubbed painfully against the lace of her bra, mimicking the way the man squeezed and pulled Marie's stiff bud as her pussy started to throb around her finger.

And it was then he saw her; she could swear those dark intent eyes looked straight at her. But she didn't care, she couldn't stop; it was far too late for that. She was panting as she pushed two fingers inside, fucking herself urgently as the two men played with Marie.

Dan reached the top of Marie's thigh again, and now he wasn't licking, he was pushing forward; his probing tongue had found the glistening pussy, Roisin gasped and Marie's soft voice broke and she was crying out, writhing frantically. God, that hard tongue had to be going deep; she was sure Marie was begging for more as Dan held her hips firm, dragging her tighter against his face, and as she screamed out. Roisin bit back her own cry and came. Came with her, gasping for breath, panting and sinking down against her hand as the soft pulsing turned to a hard throb and her pussy grabbed at her fingers, sending a rush of wetness over her hand.

She closed her eyes and sank down onto her haunches, letting her hand slip out from her tight shorts, bringing it up beside her head to support her. She curled her nails against the hard slats, the sweet smell of her own orgasm surrounding her. The tremble gradually ebbed from her body as she rested her forehead against the wood and took a deep, steadying breath. What the hell was happening to her? What was she doing in her stable yard finger-fucking herself? But all she could think of was Marie being so soundly pleasured by the two men, of the look of pure abandon on her face. Shit. Two men. Two tongues, four hands. She'd never really believed anyone actually did that, and now she wanted it.

She turned around on wobbling legs and sank down with the building against her back. Tipping her head back, she let the warmth of the sun bathe her face and took another deep breath. What was she supposed to do now? Admit she'd seen them, or run away and pretend it hadn't happened? She'd come down here for a reason, hadn't she? To talk to them, find out more about their therapy business, about what was really going on. Was she going to run away at the first glimpse of what it was all about? She couldn't back down now; she'd agreed to stay here, run her business alongside theirs. Manage them. Shit.

"You don't have to stand on ceremony, you know." The dark-haired man spoke with a soft, knowing drawl as his black eyes burned into hers. "Just pop in any time you want."

Fuck, he knew; he'd seen her watching. Fuck, fuck, fuck. Her eyes were drawn down to his hands. The hands she'd been watching. She knew she was going beetroot red. She glanced back up, daring him to say anything, but he just looked, a knowing look that set off an uncontrollable flutter deep down in her stomach.

All three of them looked respectable enough for a vicar's tea party and here she was, feeling shagged out and disheveled. And they were waiting. For her to say something, like why she was there. And all she could do was stare at them openmouthed. While he stood there smirking. Bugger.

"Come in and join us, Roisin. You've not met James yet, have you?" Dan's voice broke into the tense air that hung between them.

"You're going to love James." Marie stood up and moved over to wrap an arm around the man's slim waist, looking up at him with adoration. "He's our right-hand man, we wouldn't be without him." Double bugger.

Roisin ran her tongue nervously over her lips, instantly regretting it. She risked another look at the enigmatic James, and a sudden grin broke the aquiline features, softening them. Right-hand man just about summed it up, unless you included the left as well. Which, to be fair, they probably should.

"We've been filming a video." James's soft voice was as sensual as the touch of his hands had been and she was suddenly struck by how like a panther he was. Dark, graceful, and hidden. Something about him gave the impression you'd never know what he really was, who he was. He was watching her closely, and she knew her nipples were tweaking out at him, blaring out their own "touch me, touch me" invitation.

"A video about just how much you can turn a woman on without even having sex," James continued. "But I think you understand that bit, don't you?" She was sure he was laughing at her, and Dan was looking from one to the other as though he could sense the undercurrent between them. She felt a shiver run through her. What would it feel like to have Saul sucking her pussy, kneeling between her legs as James sucked her breasts, teased her just as she'd watched him tease Marie?

"Stop it, James." Marie swatted at him affectionately and moved over to take her hand and pull her farther into the room. "If it wasn't for Roisin we'd still be stuck in no-hope land."

"Ah, so this is the famous Roisin, and I thought it was just some girl looking for riding lessons." Roisin felt the heat burn through her as James's gaze wandered over her body as though he was working out just which bits of her needed attention.

"Stop it, James." Marie shook her head. "Not everyone gets your teasing, you know. Ignore him." She smiled at Roisin again and pushed a chair in her direction. "I keep telling him his charms don't work on everyone."

Mmm, charms, is that what they were called?

"Sorry." James grinned and held out a hand, but he didn't look sorry. She stared at the hand, the hand she had just seen work its magic over Marie. She wasn't sure she wanted to touch him. She gave in; she had to let him touch her, and it wasn't that bad. It wasn't that shock she got every time Saul touched her; it was just a warmth, a lulling warmth that held a promise of satisfaction, a growing heat of pure promise. She grabbed her hand back and stuck it behind her back, ignoring his look. "I'm just a man for hire, I guess." Which took her right back to thoughts of brothels. And why this wouldn't work.

"He's actually really experienced," Marie said.

Oh yeah?

"He's so good with people. They all love him. He can tell exactly what someone wants and then explain to their partner how to give it to them. God knows how he does it." Marie was twittering on like so much background noise, and Roisin had to force herself to concentrate on the words.

James was still smiling a lazy smile at her, his head tipped. "Just a knack, I guess." He was the type of man you could love or hate. Her stomach tightened. The type of man who could give you pleasure but not love. A panther. She watched his face as she wetted her suddenly dry lips. She should have met him at the bar the other day, not Saul, not a man who already seemed to be getting under her skin in a way she didn't want. "And I know exactly what you need." A panther purring before the kill.

She started guiltily, and his grin broadened. "You need a nice relaxing massage, darling."

"Yes, yes." Marie had jumped up. God, the woman was hyper;

maybe that was what lots of sex did for you. "That's a brilliant idea, James." She turned to Roisin. "He is so good at massage you wouldn't believe it; he has such good hands."

Roisin felt herself tighten protectively, she'd just seen those good hands in action.

"He is good, Roisin, believe us. No funny stuff, he just has magic hands." Dan spoke for the first time, his soft, caressing voice breaking across Marie's more excited tones. "This will be a welcome gift from us, a thank-you for having us. You'll love it." He grinned. "And you really need to sample the goods if you're going to be overseeing the business."

She tried to stop doing her best goldfish impression, but her brain wasn't cooperating and all she could do was squeak, it seemed. She didn't want a massage; she so didn't want a massage from this man.

"You guys do that while me and Marie get some stuff together," Dan said, "and then we'll show you some of our plans for this place. You're going to love it."

Love it. Christ, their enthusiasm was unending while her stomach was lurching like it didn't know what to do next, and her pussy was positively purring. But their mood was contagious; she did feel more hopeful than she had for ages. More alive in a way. Maybe something as outrageous as this was what she needed. Let her body do the talking, or walking, or whatever.

Everything in her life had always been so restrictive: her boarding school, her parents, her husband. All she'd known was expectations and proscriptions, and now this. No rules, it seemed, except the ones you wanted. For the first time, freedom. She stood up, aware of her legs still trembling. "I'm sure it will be great." Aware of the catch in her voice.

"Top off." He was standing expectantly, hands on slim hips, waiting. She eyed the padded bench; well, it was just a massage. A massage, no toe- or finger-sucking. She lay down, face-first, trying to steady her breathing as he undid the clasp on her bra and the cool air snaked around her breasts. Firm hands eased her shorts farther down onto her hips, tucking a towel into the waistband as though he did this every day. Oh hell, he couldn't smell her, could her? Smell that "I've just been fucking myself" smell?

"Relax." And then his warm hands were on her back with a touch of pure bliss as though they belonged there, and her body obeyed, even if her mind hadn't caught up yet. He stroked upward, pushed her hair to one side with almost a lover's caress, gentle and caring but a whisper away from sensual. Firm thumbs pressed up her spine as though they were reaching deep into her being and she closed her eyes so that she was more aware of his touch, of the feeling of letting herself be touched just for the sake of it. Thumbs rolled deeply across her shoulders, seeking out tension she didn't know she had, the heels of his hands pressed firmly around her shoulder blades, across her back, and all she could hear was his steady, soothing breathing as she let her body sink deeper. His hand traveled lower, his thumb rubbing slow, firm circles at the base of her spine until she could feel the sensation spread down between her cheeks, feel the warmth build between her legs, the dampness build again in her pussy. But she couldn't move, didn't want to tense, just let the feelings build, swirl. His hands trailed slowly up her sides, skimming the sides of her breasts, leaving a tingle of awareness as he skated inward over her back again, large, sweeping motions that one second teased and tantalized, and the next moment soothed and caressed.

"Do you want me to carry on?" His soft voice was in her ear, but far away, and she knew she gave only the slightest nod, not wanting him to stop; this was too nice. This was heaven without the fight to get there. Strong fingertips circled over her muscles, deeper, lighter, until her body responded, lifting and falling in time. So lightly she almost thought she imagined it, he traced small circles over the sensitive skin of her waist, sending tingles down her spine, all the way deep into her core. Heat emanated outward until it surged through her body. She heard a murmur of pleasure she knew came from her, felt him move closer to her. His featherlight touch on her waist deepened, his hand drifted firmly in, down her spine, pressing more firmly until she could feel her pussy start to throb, feel the waves spread as she relaxed her legs and felt them fall farther apart. His soft, damp lips were on her back, his tongue making a trail down her spine, then back up, tasting her, sucking her skin, his thumbs circling, fingers massaging. And then the soft waves that had been building started to roll through her body and it felt like her pussy was opening up with each pulse, the orgasm spreading to every bit of her. She was dimly aware of him pulling the towel higher over her back, dimly aware of his murmur soft against her cheek. Then nothing mattered anymore.

"Hey, dozy, I think you needed that."

Roisin's eyes flew open and she went to sit up, but Marie put a steadying hand on her. "Whoa, slow down or you'll get dizzy. James said you were out like a light as soon as he finished. Some people do that." Marie gave a friendly grin. "He's got magic hands, hasn't he? We're in the office when you're ready."

Magic hands. That was one way of describing them. She'd just had an orgasm. A mind-blowing, rolling, whole body orgasm with a man she was fairly sure she didn't fancy, and he hadn't touched a single erogenous zone on her body. Well, definitely not any of the obvious ones. And now she felt spaced out.

She reached back to do her bra up and then sat up gingerly. She did feel spaced out—spaced out and utterly relaxed, like she'd done a hard day's work then had a good night's sleep.

◦◦◦

"Better?" Three pairs of eyes were on her as she walked into the office she'd once called her own.

"Much, er, thanks." Yay, she was much, much better.

"You need one of those every week; I'll put you in the diary, shall I? Perk of the job?" James sat studying her through hooded eyes that almost saw too much, but he'd lost the smart-ass edge, looked ever so slightly less the predator.

"Thanks, yes, it was great." As long as he didn't mind her rolling over and begging for more next time.

Dan looked up from his laptop. "Maybe you should bring Saul along next time." She felt the warmth creep into her face. Why the hell did she feel guilty? His tone was open, deceptively light, and she wasn't quite sure if it was directed at her or James.

"I'm not sure he'll be around."

"Oh? I got the impression he was going to be sticking around. I thought you two—?"

"Us two? We're not a couple." They weren't. He'd made that

more than clear, hadn't he? Not that she wanted to be part of a couple, not that it had ever been anything more than a one-night stand that had stretched into two, that had morphed into a business agreement that would tie them together for months. Bugger.

"Really?"

This was getting annoying; she would not be lumped together with him and if, for some weird reason, that's what they thought, then they had better stop. "Really."

There was one of those glances that flicked between Marie and Dan and she could feel herself getting all prickly inside.

James stood up. "I'll be back later, guys, I'll leave you three to"—he quirked an eyebrow—"work things out."

"Look, Roisin, I'm not trying to interfere here, but the way he was looking at you yesterday…"

"It's business. We've—you know, but now it's just business, okay?"

Dan raised an eyebrow. "You know?"

Why did everyone in a couple always think that was what the rest of the world wanted or needed? Unless…She paused. Unless something else was bothering him? "Look, I'm sorry, but you're just working with me. Saul is out of the picture. Is that a problem?"

"No." Dan shrugged, his voice as even as ever. "Not a problem. It's just…" He seemed to hesitate, glanced over at Marie as though to get her permission to continue. "It's just we know Saul quite well, we like him, and…"

"And the way he was with you seemed to be more than just a 'you know.'" Marie finished the sentence.

"You're wrong." Her voice sounded taut even to her own ears, but they were wrong. She knew. Anything more would have been wrong for both of them. She needed to be in control of her own life for once, and he'd made it more than clear that he didn't want any ties. No promises. No hanging around.

"Sorry, then, our mistake."

"But you do know him, don't you? What was that video I saw all about, the one of him spanking his wife?"

"You'll have to ask him, Roisin. He was our client and we don't discuss what happens in sessions. It's a matter of confidentiality. Sorry, but I'm sure you understand."

"But you said you knew him well."

"We knew him as a client, and then when things went belly-up he just happened to be the first person who came along. We discussed the business with him, but he didn't think he could take it on, didn't think he could help."

"Until he got this place?"

"Until he met you. It wasn't the place that gave him the idea. It was you, Roisin."

"Rubbish." She bit her lip; whatever he was playing at, it wasn't being cozy with her.

"You know it's not rubbish. Saul might be a hard-nosed businessman, but he's not ruthless. He wanted to help us, and I think he wants to help you. He could have easily broken this place up, sold it for redevelopment, and made a killing."

"I know." That was the bit that really bothered her. "So why didn't he?"

"Exactly. You tell us."

She sank down into the chair. "I don't know, but he's moved on, gone." *Probably because I told him I don't trust him.* She looked from one half of the couple to the other and saw something that could have been sympathy. "I want to work this out, I want to keep my home, and he's thrown me a lifeline and that's all I know. I don't know why he's doing it, but it's not because there's something between us; it's really not. I want us to get on and make a go of this, and it isn't just because I want to keep the place. I like you." She shrugged; she did like them, and already she felt like she'd known them for years. "I don't know a thing about your business but I want to, and maybe"—she glanced down self-consciously and then back up to meet Dan's gaze—"maybe you can help me out a bit too. I think I need educating."

The self-deprecating laugh rang out and for a moment they just looked. Something gripped at her stomach; were they going to say it wouldn't work? Did they want Saul here as well; was that the deal they'd bought into?

"That's fine." Dan stood up and moved over to put an arm around Marie. "We like you too, Roisin, you're good, alone or with Saul. Though I think you're wrong about him." He paused and they swapped that look again. "But we usually help couples together; we're all about couples, really." He shrugged and looked down to Marie for her to finish off what he was saying.

"But, before, I, um…"

"Ah." He smiled, as if reading her mind. "What you saw was something quite a few couples fantasize about, a third person joining them, but that's about consent, that's about them both wanting it. We do it quite a lot because we both like it, Roisin, although we're never unfaithful, and what James told you before was right. That was a video aimed at showing pleasure without penetration." She felt herself squirm inside slightly at his matter-of-fact tone. "We just thought we'd make it more interesting by adding in a few things like an extra man, like the ties."

"It's not that I want"—oh, life must be so much easier if you're not a prude—"a threesome or anything. I just meant it's not just couples, I just thought if you did…"

"We want to make people's sex lives better, and that means different things to different people, but it isn't about a step-by-step guide to orgasm." He sighed.

"I know, I've just never…Before Saul I…"

"We can help you find out about yourself and what you want, but the hardest part is telling someone else, hun, which is why if Saul…" Marie was looking at her as if she got it, but she didn't. As though the only solution was Saul. Which figured, seeing as she'd never had a man bring her to a knee-trembling orgasm before she met him.

"No." Her abruptness surprised even her, and she forced a softer tone into her voice. "No, it's me, just me, and I don't need anyone else right now. Saul and I haven't got a problem because there is no Saul and I." A phone rang out into the silence, and it took a moment for her to register that it was hers.

Saul.

"I think we need to talk. I've changed my mind."

Chapter 8

"Sorry, what do you mean you've changed your mind?"

"We'll talk when I get there. I'm on my way back, be with you in a couple of hours." The rich, deep voice crept along her skin. "I thought I'd give you warning this time." He gave a short laugh, setting off the memory of the last time he'd come back unexpectedly, a thought that sent a tingle of anticipation straight between her thighs. Two days without him and the sound of his voice took her right back to square one. Even though what he was saying, what he was doing, didn't make sense.

"Considerate of you." The tightness in her throat gave her words an edge she hadn't meant.

"I thought so, although I'd be quite happy to catch you unawares again." The dry tone hit a nerve it shouldn't have.

"I'm with Dan and Marie." She was sure they could hear every word; though, to be fair, what was a bit of eavesdropping after what she'd been doing?

"Still? Don't you have your own business to run as well?" He was definitely sounding edgy.

"I'm quite capable of managing my own time, thanks." She couldn't stop the sigh. "I thought you had some work down there you had to sort? Why are you heading back? I don't get it."

"Sorted for now. I need to check some things with Dan." Ah,

so that put her in her place. He was heading back for Dan, and needed a bed for the night.

"I think I'll have to start charging you B and B fees." It was meant to lighten the tone, but went down like the proverbial lead balloon.

"I'm sure we can come to an arrangement. Right, traffic is busy so I better go. See you soon."

There was a clunk and then she was left with the dull tone of nothing. "He's on his way." As though they didn't know. And he'd already managed to twist her body back into the ball of tension it had been before James had worked his magic on it.

—⁓—

"What did you mean, you've changed your mind?"

"What were you doing with Dan and Marie?" He had his hands jammed in his pockets and he looked almost as though he were gunning for a fight. "And James?" Which was daft, except for the way he said it, and the way he stood, hands by holsters.

"I was finding out about the business, of course." She took a half step away. "If I'm going to manage it I have to understand it. Now tell me what you meant."

"No, you don't have to understand anything. They're doing the day-to-day stuff; all you were supposed to be involved in was the facilities management, sort out any problems."

"That's not how I work; I want to understand. Anyway, you've changed your tune."

"No, I haven't. I told you already, they know what they're doing."

"What's this about, Saul? Why have you suddenly come back after pissing off and telling me you were too busy?"

"I haven't suddenly come back. I always intended keeping an eye on things and it's early days, but I'm not sure it's going to work."

"Eye on things? Or on me? So you don't trust me to run the place? Is that what you're saying?"

"I didn't say that." He stopped his pacing abruptly and raked her with a stare that would have sent her back another step if she didn't already know him, and wasn't gritting her teeth, determined to hold her ground.

"Well, you either trust me or you don't, and from where I'm standing…"

He took a sharp step toward her and the words froze between them. Whatever had gotten into him, it wasn't good.

"Trust? Well we know your stance on that, don't we? And why should I trust your business decisions when I hardly know you?"

"And I hardly know you, and will you stop trying to intimidate me?" She wasn't going to step back; she rooted herself, forcing her breathing to stay steady. She'd never run from anyone before and she wasn't about to start now.

"Huh, if you think this is intimidation…" He was inches from her, his breathing heavy and his eyes burning into her with an intensity he'd not shown before. "Have you found out enough about them to satisfy you now, then?" It seemed to be taking him an effort to stay this controlled.

She dropped her gaze to the pulse in his jaw. "I've only just started." She knew she shouldn't goad him, knew it was a mistake, but she couldn't help herself.

"Oh really?" His voice was a deliciously soft warning. "And what's next in your exploration?"

"You've been spying on me."

"Me?" He gave a short laugh. "I don't spy on anyone, darling, and I want an answer. Who are you going to attend riding lessons with next?"

"Bastard." He caught her wrist even before she really realized she'd swung at him, stopping her hand inches from its mark. "Don't be crude, and it's none of your business anyway." She bit the inside of her lip, aware of just how close he was.

"And what if I'm making it my business?"

"Well, don't. You might control the business but you don't control me."

"Really?" There was the faintest of twists to his lips and then, without warning, she'd been dragged closer, his fingers twisting themselves in her hair as his mouth came down brutally hard on hers. She opened her mouth to speak but she couldn't; he was pushing her lips farther apart with a tongue that forced the musky taste of his arousal straight to the core of her. He pulled back, his eyes almost black. She gasped for air, brushing across her tingling lips with fingers that trembled.

"You, you…" This time she hit her mark, her fist thumping into his ribs, and his jaw clenched in response. She swung again, but there was no second chance; he was ready, and he caught her wrist effortlessly.

"I thought I warned you not to start a fight with me you couldn't finish."

"You bastard."

"You said it." He grabbed her other wrist, pinning them both above her head against the wall that he had backed her into.

Saul looked straight into those flashing eyes and realized he'd never seen anyone look so shaggable. Roisin was panting, her mouth slightly open, her cheeks flushed pink, her hair tangled around her shoulders.

The text from Dan had sparked something in him that he didn't get, and he hadn't been able to control. The thought of her there, talking about sex with them, about her lying on a table while James massaged his way into her mind, had sent every other thought spinning out of his own. Even though he knew it was only business. Even though he knew there was nothing wrong. Even though he knew he should stay away.

The latest business plan hadn't mattered; only the image of her there naked, the image of her aroused body shifting under James's hands had mattered. James, the man he had never planned on seeing again. The man who wasn't supposed to be there.

And now she was spitting at him like an angry cat defending its patch and the sight was sending a sharp stab of need straight to his cock.

Her breasts lifted and fell with her unsteady breathing, her nipples sharply outlined against the thin cotton, and he had to see her now, here. He reached back, got his knife from his back pocket, watched her eyes flash, widen as he flicked the blade open. So she thought she didn't trust him?

For a second he paused, letting her feel the cold of the blade against her skin, and then slowly, deliberately he let the sharpness slice open the T-shirt, watched the material peel slowly open in front of his eyes from neck to waist as she froze, her gaze locked with his, her nipples peaking ever harder.

She let out the sharp intake of breath, her swollen lips parting farther until he could see the damp tip of her tongue, feel the sweetness of her breath. Slowly he turned the knife, let the cold handle trace a path between the full breasts, down over the tight stomach, watching her clench each muscle in response, imagining her clenching the muscles in her pussy in time. Fuck, he could almost feel that sweet cunt tightening around him.

Her eyes had darkened, the black pupil widening with want until it almost flooded the emerald green away, until all he could see was want, need, and his own stomach clenched in response sending a dull ache spiraling down to his balls.

He spun her around, pushing the side of her face against the wall, pulled her arms down and around her back, and stripped the torn T-shirt over her shoulders and down until he could use it to tie her wrists. She gasped, licking her lips, waiting, needing, and all it took was one touch of his hand between her thighs for her to open up for him.

She was perfect. He stared, taking in the slim waist, the bound wrists. The tight white jodhpurs hugged every toned inch of her bum and thighs, the long black leather boots wrapped around her calves, and he felt a new rush of blood to his already engorged cock.

He swallowed hard, feeling the ache build, feeling control start to spin away. The blade of the knife slid under her waistband, sliced through the thin material of her riding jodhpurs until all he could see was the black lace of the thong that nestled between the soft roundness of her buttocks. She gasped as the cool metal slid under the thin scrap of material and one flick of his wrist broke through it. She was his, and he was going to have her. He let the knife drop from his fingers, heard the heavy clunk as it hit the floor, his hand already on his zipper as his other reached down between her thighs. She was panting, rocking, as he met the unresisting softness of a pussy that ran with juices, juices he could smell, a sweetness he could almost taste. And then he had his hands on the soft swell of her hips, his thumbs digging into the plumpness of her bum, and he watched as his swollen cock slid right in where it belonged. Her moan nearly sent him over the edge with that first slow glide in. He felt her grasping at him, her slickness coating him; could feel her throbbing that he needed so much to be his own, and then he couldn't hold back any longer. He hammered into her, heard the grunt that turned to a moan, then she was shouting out his name and his body took over from his mind. All he could think of was taking every inch of her, branding her, filling her. She spread her legs wider, sank down as he pounded upward. The sound of her yelling and begging for more filled his head; as his balls nestled against the warm wetness, he heard a sound that had to be him, and then he'd lost it.

She eased herself away from the wall and slowly turned to face him. For a moment they just stared at each other. She pulled awkwardly, trying to loosen her arms, which were still bound behind her back.

"Are you going to untie me, then?" The husky note of her voice swirled at the base of his stomach and he shook his head slowly.

"Oh no, we're not done yet." His voice matched hers as he fought to steady his breathing, and he knew he was far from done. She'd gotten under his skin and he didn't know how to stop her, didn't know how to put things back to normal. Not until they'd done what they had to and broken whatever kind of spell had them in its grip. He ran one hand down the side of her face and she twisted her head to kiss his hand, then she slowly licked down the length of it, sucking the mound at the base of his thumb, those green eyes fixed on him all the time.

"Witch." She shivered; she wanted it too, wanted to fuck until it was out of their systems, until it was over. He ran his hand down her neck, watched the goose bumps rise on her skin, drifted down until he had her breast cradled. His thumb teased over her nipple, making it harden. "We're nowhere near done yet."

He let his hands drift down over her silky skin, rubbed his thumbs just inside her hip bones, watching the shudder run through her body, and then he shifted his hands just enough to lift her. She was light, but it wouldn't have made any difference if she hadn't been as he carried her up the stairs and laid her gently down in the middle of the bed. He was going to sort this if it killed him.

"James turned you on, didn't he?"

Roisin shivered as his hand slowly traced a path down the side of her body, the back of his fingers warm and smooth against the dip of her waist. He sat astride her legs, pulled her against his body and, with one motion, freed her wrists. As he laid her back she reached up instinctively. Firm fingers danced up the delicate inner skin of her outstretched arms, stopping abruptly at her wrists. Pinning her back down against the mattress.

"Exactly where I want you, darling." The wolfish grin made her nipples peak as he drew her wrists closer, binding them together before fastening them to the headboard so that her breasts lifted. Shit, the man was a control freak, not that she was going to pretend being tied up didn't do it for her. He edged down her body, leaned forward, and she groaned as his tongue circled her nipple. Hard teeth slid along the delicate skin, burning a trail of sensation that stopped abruptly as his gaze met hers. "You liked the way he touched you, didn't you?"

Fuck, why couldn't he just shut up? "Is that what this is about?" She gasped as he ran his hand into the indent of her waist, the rough tips of his fingers grazing her skin.

"Do you think of his hands on your skin when I touch you?"

"Who?"

He glared and she shook her head.

"No." A small whisper in the large room that should have echoed. "No, I was thinking about you when he touched me."

He ran a firm hand over her thigh. Her muscles tensed as he reached her knee, circled, and then traced back up the inside. Her legs clamped tight together as a wave of need traveled up to her pussy and he laughed, rolling off the bed.

"Oh, no, Roisin, it's my turn to be in control, my turn to decide if you're allowed to be greedy." His hand tugged firmly at her ankle, sliding her body down taut over the satin sheets before he tied it securely, his burning gaze never leaving her as he walked around to the other side of the bed. Her muscles clenched, resisting as he pulled her legs apart, her body tightening against the firm strength as his eyes narrowed slightly and sent new heat straight to her pussy. He shook his head slowly. "You won't win, not this time." The dark head bent closer, his tongue tracing a damp path along her hot pussy, making her whimper. "But you don't want to, do you, darling?"

She shook her head. She should mind, she really should mind

being pinned to the bed, but she didn't. She wanted to be here, waiting to see what he did to her next.

"All those dirty thoughts running around in your head, but you don't know what you want, do you? You're not going to admit to wanting another man, are you?" She squirmed as much as the bindings would allow, her skin tingling at his smile. "I want you to be honest, Roisin. I need you to be honest with me."

"I am honest. How did you know he…?" Her voice was a rasp in the silence and she swallowed to clear her throat. His finger suddenly sank into her slickness and she closed her eyes at the hard, blissful intrusion, lifting her hips, a gentle ripple of orgasm instantly rolling through her body.

"James turned you on, didn't he?" He was twisting his finger inside her, creating a new wave of want, and it didn't matter that he hadn't answered her question.

"Yes." *Please don't stop, please don't stop.*

"He made you all wet, didn't he?" His finger rolled up inside her, curling rhythmically against her G-spot with the slightest tormenting pressure. "Didn't he?"

"Yes." She was panting, clenching her muscles as he held her there on the edge of orgasm. "Please."

"Open your eyes. Look at me." She ran her tongue over her lips, opened her eyes to meet his gaze, and for a moment didn't know what she was seeing. He was staring intently, his expression a mix of desire and something she didn't understand. "He's going to give you the type of private lesson you're not going to forget, Roisin." She cried out as he squeezed his thumb down hard against the swollen bud of her clit, a clit that was already throbbing to the point where she couldn't distinguish between pain and pleasure.

"Because that's what you want, my little greedy girl, isn't it?" His voice was soft in her ear as he built the pleasure relentlessly.

"I don't…" She lifted her hips to follow his hand, her legs trembling.

"You do, Roisin. Look." She followed his gaze then, freezing as she noticed the figure in the doorway. How long had he been there? Had he been watching her as she'd watched him earlier? "Do you want him to touch you?"

Shit, she couldn't say no; her whole body was crying out to feel those hands on her again, even as she was clenching around Saul's fingers. Just seeing him standing there, his black eyes raking over her body, was sending new shudders through her.

The warm touch of his hand on her foot sent an electric jolt through her body, even though she could see him, even though she knew he was going to do it. She gasped as his thumb pressed into the arch of her foot, and her legs fought against the ties as her inner thighs tightened around Saul's hand. He slowly drew his fingers down, leading a damp trail of her juices against her thigh, and for a second she saw the two men share a look before he reached to the side of the bed for something, and then his hand was under her head, lifting her, and she realized what he was doing just as the blindfold came down, blocking her vision.

Chapter 9

"JAMES IS HERE BECAUSE I asked him, Roisin, not as a member of staff. He can do whatever you want him to. Is that okay? Say now if you don't want this?" His voice was soft silk in her ear; his lips drifted across her, warming her cheek before settling on her mouth. Teeth nibbled across her lower lip, pulling, tugging gently until she opened her lips, and then he molded his own over hers, easing until she opened her mouth wider, until he could explore with his tongue. He circled around her teeth, setting alight new sensation before plunging deeper so that she could taste him, taste his lust, her whole body softening in response.

A sudden thrust inside her pussy set her body taut against the ties in shock, and she fought to jerk away from the demanding mouth, tried to cry out. But the sound was lost in his mouth as his strong hands held her head firm, and his tongue plunged deeper into her throat. Fingers on her hips dug in, and as her body accepted the intrusion she realized it was a tongue, probing, lapping, thrusting, and fluttering in time.

Saul's bruising lips softened against hers and he drew her tongue into his mouth, sucking softly, persistently, until she started to unravel. And as she did, as her thighs started to melt against the bed, James started to suck on her throbbing clit. She moaned into Saul's mouth and her body must have given in to

James's because he nuzzled deeper, sucking harder until her hips started to buck. Abruptly he stopped, and then started to lap at her soaking cunt with long strokes that made her body rock, until it felt like she was opening up, breaking apart, and he slipped a long finger inside her.

"That's nice, isn't it?" Saul had released her mouth, his breath still on her face, one hand moving down to cup her breast. She gasped as he tweaked her nipple between thumb and forefinger before gently starting to roll it, then pull it gently to an ever-hardening peak, and all the time there was the finger sliding in and out of her pussy. He was rubbing lightly against her G-spot with each stroke, her pussy trembling with each touch.

And Saul's finger was circling, teasing her nipple, tearing her mind between the two sensations as a whimper built in her throat. Warmth wrapped around her other breast; a hand that felt so different, a warming, caressing hand that kneaded and pulled as it matched the movement deep in her pussy.

Her stomach clenched, tightening in response to the ripples that ran through her with each new sensation, and she pulled against the bindings, trying to lift her hips, to press her clit against the teasing hand. Then a sudden jolt of awareness shot straight down to the engorged bud as two mouths closed around her full, heavy breasts. Two grasping, sucking mouths that bathed her with their warmth, that made her cunt clench around the finger as her boobs were sucked in deeper, sucked until she was on the edge of pain and a cry was ripped from her. She needed so desperately to clutch her thighs together and bring herself to the orgasm that she was hesitating on the brink of. But she couldn't. She rolled her hips desperately, and then there was new pressure against her cunt; two, three fingers thrusting inside her, another hand rubbing against her swollen, oversensitized nub. The twin mouths softened against her breasts, tongues lapping at her nipples, teeth teasing. As the hand thrust harder inside her dripping core, as the pressure increased on her clit, she dimly heard her voice scream out Saul's name before her whole body convulsed with an intense rush of pleasure that left her fighting for breath.

"Shh." Damp hands were stroking lightly over her thighs, fingers tangling in her hair, lips caressing her stomach as the waves slowly ebbed in her body. As the final shudders left her, the ties were loosened so that she could bring her shaking limbs together. She rolled to one side, her arms reaching for the reassuring strength of what she knew was Saul's body and, as he peeled the blindfold off, she closed her eyes and let him pull her close.

Soft lips were pressed against her forehead as his hand skated down her side to settle at her waist. "We've not finished yet though, darling." She groaned and his chuckle wrapped around her senses, making her tingle in a way she wouldn't have thought she had the energy for. The bed dipped behind her, the weight of a hand settled on her hip just below Saul's and she shifted uneasily, straight against a hard cock, the tip damp against her back. She froze, and James moved closer, his breath warm against her neck.

"And now which way are you going to go, missy?" The damp-ness of his tongue against her neck was almost soothing and she stretched out, tilting her head so that he could access her skin all the way from the dip of her shoulder up to a spot just behind her ear. This was nice, sensual but soothing, and she wrapped her legs over Saul's so she could nestle her hips closer against his. His semihard dick twitched against her uncovered mound, its tip velvet smooth and hot as she lifted her pelvis so that he slipped down between her legs, nudging against her swollen lips. His chuckle reverberated through his body, through hers. She wanted him, wanted to feel him inside her, and she hooked her legs tighter around his body, pulling him tighter to her as she rocked her hips, trying to tease the tip of him inside, her cunt clutching with need as James's hard dick nudged against her bum.

He rolled onto his back then, taking her with him, sliding her forcefully over him so her slick cunt sheathed his cock in one easy movement that made her gasp. She needed to slide against his body, grate her clit against his hard pelvis, but he held her tight, still with firm hands on her hips so that all she could feel was him twitching, growing inside her. She groaned and rocked her body, grinding down against him, watching his nipples harden into tight beads, and then he was pulling her down and James was easing her feet down, stretching her legs wide so she was spread until she could hardly move. She could squeeze her pussy, though, and rock against him despite his firm grip on her hips. She stared into Saul's eyes as she throbbed around him and the dark lust in them spread like a fire through her.

His jaw was set, his lips tight with self-control, control she wanted to shatter, and he seemed to read it in her face because he was shaking his head. "Not yet, Roisin." As the soft voice reached her a cold splash on her buttocks made her clench in surprise, then a finger was spreading what had to be oil or gel between her cheeks. Warming it, pressing it between her cheeks, around her back passage. She clenched again, and he rubbed with two fingers, spreading her cheeks, circling her hole.

"I want to fuck this lovely ass." James's voice startled her even though she knew he was there, knew his fingers were on her bum. She gasped as he pressed more firmly against her, circling, trying to ease his way past the ring of muscle that she clenched automatically. He pressed more firmly, widening her hole, edging inside her.

Shit, that felt good, good in a way it shouldn't. She groaned as Saul shifted her slightly, took her nipple between his fingers. He squeezed hard and she cried out at the sudden pain that shot through her on a route straight to her clit. And as he let go and she relaxed, the firm finger pushed its way past her defenses, knuckle-deep into her ass. The heat built in her pussy as the finger slid in and out, and as Saul eased her back and forward around his hard cock. James pulled out and she mewed out an objection before gasping as he pressed back firmer, trying to edge her wider with two fingers.

"Push down against him, darling, open up for him." She shut her eyes as Saul pulled her body tight against his, rubbing her taut nipples against the roughness of his chest until every nerve ending seemed to be responding. James had moved and, for a moment, she felt abandoned, strangely exposed, until he leaned back in close, his hard cock pressed against her.

"I can't..." She tensed up at the pressure.

"You can, Roisin, You want both of us filling you, don't you? Don't you want that?" Saul's breath bathed her neck, sending a shiver of anticipation. Firm fingers were massaging the base of her spine; small, persistent circles that set her skin shivering as they traced down. The strong pressure made her pussy throb with need.

"I want, I want..." She was gasping against his mouth, breathing in the smell of his arousal, of hers, feeling his cock nudging against her G-spot as he slid her back and forth with painful precision. "Yes, I want both of you."

His fingers meshed in her hair, pulled her down until the warmth of his mouth enveloped hers. The hungry intensity sent her senses tumbling; a new need, a greed that seemed to reach out and draw her deep into him. And as their mouths melded, her body relaxed and opened up. There was burning pain as James pushed into her, and still he was massaging, rubbing until the tight ring of muscle relaxed again and he could push deeper, deeper. She swore she could feel their two cocks rubbing against each other, swore she was about to burst with the fullness as they rocked her between them. A hard thrust sent pain and pleasure reeling through her as James's fingers dug into her ass, and the moan inside her mouth told her they were all heading to a point of no return. She could feel his balls against her as he thrust in, feel the fullness of Saul surge deeper as she was pulled back.

She had to come; each hard, burning thrust that James made was pushing her forward, her swollen clit hard against Saul. And then he was slamming her back against him, his fingers tight on her hips, the friction building the throb in her pussy and the ache deep in her belly until she thought she was going to burn up.

Her ass felt on fire, inside and out, stretching as James swelled inside her; then she could feel him coming, a wave of need flowing straight to her clit as his hands on her eased their grip. There was one groan, one final hard thrust, and her pussy was clutching Saul's dick as James pulsed inside her.

"Shit." Saul rolled her over onto her back, pounding into her with a frustration and greed that sent her whole body into a fierce convulsion, and then they were coming together, his hot come shooting into her, bathing her insides, and all she could hear was the babble of her own voice in her ears as she locked her ankles around his waist, tipping her pelvis high to accept every last drop of him.

—⁓—

"He's gone."

"Yes, he's gone." Saul pulled her tighter against him as they lay spooned together. "You've been zonked out for ages and he's never been one to outstay his welcome."

"Oh?" She pulled away from him slightly, which wasn't really what he wanted. Rolled over to face him, which he wanted even less. "What is it with you and him? You know him, don't you?"

"I know all of them."

"Yeah, but you *really* know him." She was gnawing at her lip and gazing at him as if she did trust him. Which he supposed she must after what she'd just let him do.

"My wife, Bianca, knew him." He sighed, rolling onto his back, away from those eyes. "That's how we ended up going to them for help, because she knew him."

"But?"

"But what?"

She was staring, he could tell without looking.

"But—" He took a deep breath, drew in to fill his lungs, breathed out slow to let the air drift through his body. "They were fucking around outside of lesson time."

"Oh."

"Apparently he's irresistible." He felt his face tighten, all the way from his eyebrows right down to his jaw. Yeah, he'd come back because James was irresistible. He'd come back to involve James on purpose, to prove to himself that sharing Roisin wasn't a problem, that it was just sex, that it wouldn't be another knife in his side like last time. That this pull he had back to her, this unsettled feeling that grew in his stomach when she was with other people, was just about lust. James had fucked with his head before, and this time he wanted to prove to himself it was different. That it was over before it began. Except she'd screamed his name as she'd come, wrapped her legs around his body, fallen asleep in his arms.

"So why did you bring him here?"

He looked at her then, because she didn't sound like she was accusing him of anything. "Because you wanted him." He shrugged. "Didn't you?"

"Yep." She grinned. "He's good with his hands." That grin tugged at something inside him, so that he had to smile back and pull her close again.

"Very. And his cock."

"Very." She snuggled tighter. "Thank you."

"Oh, my pleasure." He knew he sounded dry, but it had been a strange kind of pleasure giving her what she wanted. Even if he wasn't sure he'd repeat it again.

"Do you do that a lot?"

"No, now hush." Never. It was a weird kind of pain and pleasure, gifting something that hurt. Maybe that was what Bianca had been after, but she'd pushed the limits way beyond his boundaries. And had he suffered the pain with Roisin so he could punish James? Was he doing it because he knew, deep down, it was his name she'd scream? Just what was he trying to prove, and to whom?

"Well, thank you anyway, but can we just stick to us from now on?" Shit, her voice had been drifting as she spoke and she was already shifting into sleep. So what the fuck was "us"? She'd said she was glad he wasn't sticking around, said she didn't trust him. He hadn't wanted to stay, hadn't wanted her to want him.

He rolled back over, rested his chin on the top of her head so that her sweet smell invaded his senses. Felt the soft sigh of her breathing echoing through his body and wondered what came next.

―――

"Are you two trying to poke your noses in my life, then?" Some mates went back a lifetime, but he wasn't going to open up that door to Roisin. Some things were better off limits. Dan was one of them. Dan, who was looking at him with those big, innocent blue eyes under his floppy fringe. "And don't give me the angel eyes 'cause I know exactly what you're up to."

"Do you?" Dan grinned at him and pushed a mug of coffee in his direction. "Left her all well fucked and well tucked up in bed, have you?"

"Up yours." The coffee hit him where he needed it, but the spreading warmth was down to more than that. "She gets up early and sorts her horses."

"Into riding in a big way, isn't she?" The way Dan said things meant you could take them whichever way you wanted.

"Ah, so attack is your best form of defense, is it?" He smoothed a finger along the edge of the table. "Come on, mate, why did you text like that and give me the heads up on where James was going? I thought discretion was your policy."

"I thought you'd want to know."

"And what gave you that idea?"

"You." Dan was turning the coffee cup in the saucer, and Saul could almost hear his brain ticking over. "Look, Saul, I've never pried, but I know you and James have some kind of issue, and however hard you run I know there's something in that brittle shell of yours that needs Roisin."

"I don't need anyone."

"Okay, maybe 'need' is too strong a word, but I know when two people have more than just the hots for each other, Saul, and I know that there's unfinished business between you. Now, you don't want James to try to finish it for you, do you?"

The soft voice hit hard, gibed at him in a way he wasn't going to acknowledge, not to Dan, not to himself. He wasn't going there. "Don't dig."

"Saul, we've shared most things, and I've never asked you to spill what you didn't want to, but isn't it time you stopped letting Bianca fuck with your mind?"

"What's that supposed to mean?"

"She was just a bloody woman, Saul. Okay, you thought you'd landed a stunner, and she was in some ways, but she was also a spoiled bitch who was always on the lookout for a new toy to play with. She was the most conniving cow I've ever met and, believe me, I've met a few who've played the game like pros."

Saul kept his gaze fixed on the steam rolling off the coffee.

"It's time to let go, Saul."

"I let go years ago."

"Yeah, of Bianca maybe; you had to before you bloody strangled her. But you've got to let go of the rest of the emotional shit."

"You don't understand the half of it."

"Try me. Yeah, it hurts when you find out you're just a bit

of rough, and…" Saul glanced up at the hesitation and narrowed his eyes. Dan hesitating meant he was going to go too far. "You're not even good enough at the role, but that's because it wasn't you. You're not anyone's bit of rough, mate, even if we did grow up on the wrong side of the tracks. And what's wrong with that?" He shrugged his shoulders, almost in apology. Saul thought it was probably more down to relief that he hadn't gotten the expected fist in his face, than anything else. Dan knew him as well as anyone did, knew when he was close to overstepping that line. "We did good, we're here, and we've had more fun getting here than a lot of those twats with their noses stuck up their asses."

"Cool turn of phrase. There's nothing wrong with your upbringing, then."

"You know what I mean."

"I know." Saul felt the uncomfortable lump settle in his gut, the lump that said he was being pushed where he never went.

"So why can't you give her a chance?"

"Because she's one of them."

"Hey, don't be a dick. When was there a 'them'?"

"When Bianca stretched me to snapping point."

"But you didn't snap."

He had a point, though it had been close. And if he'd been thinking with his head, not his heart, and definitely not his dick, he wouldn't have been anywhere near even stretching, let alone snapping. It would have been "thanks for the party, but you're not my type."

"No I didn't, but Dad almost did." She'd scared the shit out of him, made him feel like he didn't measure up. Just like his dad had felt.

"This isn't about your dad, Saul. Just because he fucked up with your mom it doesn't mean that history is repeating. Wise up; this is different, you're different." He sighed. "Let her in a bit man, try it." His voice was soft and he held Saul's gaze. Dan meant well, Saul knew, but it was all black and white to him, happy shagging all the way.

"Not so easy when James is there hovering again. It's not happening, Dan, not a second time. And anyway, what the hell is he doing here, I thought he left?"

"He came back. Why, what does it matter?"

"You know why."

"No I don't, Saul. What is it with you and him? What happened?"

"I saw them; I knew all about him and her. It wasn't enough for her what she was doing to me; she just had to rub my bloody nose in it, try and wind me up that little bit more."

"What do you mean you saw? What did you see?"

"Them." Shit, he wasn't going through this. Not now.

"Them doing what? Oh, don't give me that look, Saul, exactly what did you see them doing? Think about it, don't say it. I don't give a shit what that crazy cow was actually doing, but ask yourself this: have you ever seen James let anyone touch him? Yeah, he touches and he's so fucking good at it he could make a nun beg, but no one touches him back. He's got issues you wouldn't want to even go near. You didn't see anything; whatever it was you thought you saw, it was just her playing mind games."

"You can't know."

"I know. Trust me."

He watched the coffee drain down Dan's throat in one long gulp, his Adam's apple bobbing.

"She was just using him as a tool against you."

"Then why did he let her?"

"'Cause that's what he does. James doesn't give a shit about anyone and what they think. He knew he wasn't doing anything wrong; it was all her, all in your mind, and I guess he figured that was between the two of you. It was up to you what you let yourself believe. Think about it, Saul. You just think about exactly what you saw."

"I think I've done enough thinking." His throat had tightened so much he could hear it in his voice.

"So why have you done this, if you really don't want her? Why not just throw her out on the street and make a killing on this place? I've seen you do it before, man, so I know you can."

"Oh, I want her, but it doesn't change the way things are."

"Try and kid me if you want, mate, but you can't kid yourself. And you want some advice?"

"Not really, but I can see that's not going to stop you." He stood up, suddenly tired with the way this was going. There were too many thoughts in his head that he didn't want to analyze.

"Don't screw around with her head, Saul; she doesn't deserve it and you won't forgive yourself if you do."

"Well, you look after her, then. I've got to go."

"Oh yeah, so where are you running off to hide now?"

"Fuck off. Dad called, said it was urgent, and you know I haven't got a choice when he does that. I don't want him doing what he did last time."

"Sure." He was being assessed, he could feel it. Then Dan shrugged and gave a half smile. "Your choice. I'll look after her, for now, this time. But then it's up to you."

Roisin was hanging over the gate, watching him, as he started the engine. "Sorry, but I've got to go. It's urgent."

"Sure."

It would have made him feel better if she'd been riled, or disappointed in him, or anything. But all she could say was "sure."

"I'll be back as soon as I can, honest." He didn't have to say it, but he wanted to. Which was new, and made the nerves flutter in his stomach. And was honest.

"Saul." He stopped the window halfway up. "I know, I trust you." And the grin she flashed made him even more worried. Now was probably the time to hang about, face up to things, but he couldn't. Not this time. He glanced down again at his phone, which was flashing yet another message from his dad. They never spoke unless they had to. When he got a message like this it meant that trouble was on its way. Big trouble.

Chapter 10

"WELL, I CAN SEE the attractions of this place." If she had hackles capable of rising, Roisin was sure hers would be right now. The drawl in his voice was enough to make her skin crawl, but the leer of a look in his eyes set her red-haired temper toggle straight to "on." Not that she agreed with all that fiery red hair stuff; after all, everyone had to blow their top once in a while, didn't they, when the steam buildup threatened to become too much?

And she had gotten better as she'd gotten older. Much better. Apart from when she met slimeballs like this, who gave you the once-over in a way that said "I can have you anytime I want, if I can be bothered, darling." Ergh. And what really got her goat was it was always the type of man who one look told you arm's length was just never going to be far enough away from. "Wouldn't touch with a ten-foot pole" was the phrase that came to mind. Which helped, because she couldn't rise to the bait when she had that image in her head.

"Yeah, I think I just discovered why you horsy types have a certain appeal."

Fuck, though, she wished she was the queen of snarky put-downs, just once. But she wasn't. Holding a pitchfork with a load of horse manure on it probably wasn't too bad as runner-up prizes went, though.

"All you need is the whip and spurs to make the perfect picture." Oh yeah, all she needed was a whip and she'd put the creep off riding for life.

Not that he'd notice; she'd just realized that he wasn't really aware of most of her at all. His eyeballs seemed to be fixed in a slightly spooky way on her breasts, twitching in a weird way as they rose and fell. Her breasts, that was, not his eyes. She'd been working fast, trying to clear the stable, and she knew she was breathing hard, which just gave him more to look at. For a second, she was tempted to jog on the spot, just to see if she could make them pop out of his head. Which was childish and asking for trouble, even if she was the one holding the pitchfork.

He finally managed to stop staring at her boobs and started to mentally nuzzle her thighs, which meant he'd gone too far. Even if she'd given up being disgusted with him and had moved on to deciding he was pathetic. Which was always better.

Damn, though, there was something tugging at the back of her brain that said she should know him, but she didn't. He was in a suit, which meant he wasn't local, but he looked more second-hand car salesman than city slicker, which meant he just couldn't be another of Toby's creditors. Unless this thing had gotten a whole lot seedier than she'd realized, which, given the solicitor's frown and everything she'd learned in the past few weeks, was a distinct possibility.

But she'd thought Saul had sorted all that out. Saul. Shit. All of a sudden, it hit her. This toe rag reminded her of Saul in some strange, none-too-complimentary way. "I take it you're not here to look at the horses?"

He gave a gruff laugh that said she was deranged. "Correct,

darling. Martin Mathews." His eyes flicked to her face, for what she was sure was the first time since he'd stepped in the yard, and she guessed he was looking for an appropriate reaction. Which he wasn't going to get. "And I guess you, my darling, are my son's latest victory shag. Mrs. Rosie Grant, I presume?"

She could kick him where it hurt, or empty a barrow load of what a horse did best over him. Or practice yogic breathing and pray for karma. Which could be messy, if karma in his case meant what she hoped it meant.

"Sorry?" What was it they said about being able to pick your friends and not your family? She'd thought her father had been bad enough, but Saul, it seemed, had picked more than the short straw. Some gene pools were murkier than others.

"Oh, don't be sorry." He was doing it again, mentally stripping her; obviously eye contact wasn't his thing at all. "I came to find out what the holdup is. He should be back sorting out the next deal, not dipping his wick, but I suppose I can see why he was tempted to draw this one out."

"You, he, what the—? Dipping his what?" It was a joke, he was a joke, and she must be dreaming or hallucinating or something.

"Saul always did like the perks of the job; must be his way of sealing the deal. Leaving his mark on the place—or in the place, should I say?" He was obviously pleased with that one by the resulting guffaw and the way he turned a darker shade of puce, which would have made her nervous once, before the last few surreal weeks. Now she just felt damn angry. "Though I must admit you're not his normal type. Bianca was a real glamour-puss, all long nails and a good pair of tits. Proper posh totty, if you know what I mean."

Which was her definition of something a long way from posh. "I'm afraid I don't, no." Shit, this was Toby all over again. She felt her throat closing up. Toby's taste had definitely run to talons and tits, and not hers. And so, it seemed, did Saul's.

"I suppose a change is as good as a rest. Maybe he just fancied a roll in the hay, rough with the smooth and all that." He leaned farther over the stable door to get a last good eyeful, then moved back a fraction and stuck his hands in his pockets. "Well, whatever story he told you to get into your panties I'm here to tell you the party is over, love. It's time to pack your cases."

The tone of his voice had shifted, and suddenly this wasn't the faintest bit funny anymore. "Pack?" She felt a stab of something cold and unwelcome in the pit of her stomach and had a sudden pang for the return of leering and unwelcome advances. Those she could deal with. "Look, I haven't the foggiest what all this has got to do with you even if you are Saul's dad, but I want you to go." She was glad she hadn't put the fork down because it was something to hang on to and was helping contain the tremble she could feel in her hands, a tremble she didn't want to spread to the rest of her body.

"Oh, I'm not going anywhere; we spent months putting this deal together so I'm not dropping it for anyone or anything, love."

"What deal? You didn't, I know you didn't…"

"Didn't what?"

"Spend months doing anything. Saul just spotted the opportunity, then came in and bought off the debt."

"Is that what he told you?" The mirthless laugh sent a warning curdle of something unpleasant straight to the pit of her stomach. "Well, kudos to him; he knows exactly how to get what he wants.

Sorry to burst the bubble, love, but we watched those debts pile up, we were just waiting for the right time, and if I'd had my way you would have been out before the ink on that death certificate had dried. Too soft by half, he is. You make opportunities, not wait for them in this game."

"What do you mean, make opportunities?"

"You ask, Saul, love. I'm sure he'll oblige."

She could feel a chill start to spread through her. So she'd been had. Well and truly had. She'd known there was something that didn't ring true, had put it down to the feeling between them, the strange business, everything but what it really was. She'd blanked off that instinct, the feeling in her gut. All because she couldn't keep her hands off him. Except… "We've got an agreement. I've signed an agreement." She'd signed; it was done, agreed. Whatever role his father played in all this, surely he couldn't alter that fact. "Ask him."

"What agreement?" His eyes had narrowed, but at least he'd stopped leering. "What do you mean, an agreement? He's got no right to agree anything with you."

"I've got every right." She couldn't have ignored that voice if her life had depended on it, couldn't have stopped her nipples tingling with awareness. Couldn't help the way every single erogenous zone on her body seemed to ooze to attention.

Mathews didn't even turn around, but she couldn't help it. Not that it mattered what she did; he wouldn't have noticed if she'd stripped naked and done a jig, his whole attention was on his father. Though she hardly wanted to strip, or jig, not now she'd just found out that he'd been playing some kind of game with her. She definitely didn't want to, not at all.

"I was just telling the happy hooker here how you can't resist trying out the goods every time."

That man was so fucking unpleasant.

"Dad." The low growl was a warning. "What the hell are you doing here?"

"Business. I'm here sorting out your business, Saul, because you're letting your bloody dick lead the way again." He turned around to face his son then, and Roisin suddenly felt her stomach tighten, not sure whether she was worried or excited about the tension in the air. "I came to finish off the job that you can't."

"Stop talking bollocks."

"Bollocks yourself. You just can't resist these posh birds, can you? Knowing what your fucking whore of a mother did to us wasn't enough for you, was it? Oh no, you think you're better than me, but Bianca knew just what you were, didn't she? Took you for a ride, and now you're letting another one do it. Don't you ever learn?"

Roisin couldn't help but stare at Saul, at the taut line of his jaw, the muscle that twitched just under the surface. His arms were tense—hell, his whole body was tense—but he just stood there. When he could be taking a swing. Not that she approved of that type of thing, but boy, was she tempted to offer him the pitchfork.

"Finished? Right, this is my business decision to make and I've made it." He took a step forward and Roisin moved back involuntarily. Shit, she was getting scared even if his dad wasn't. It was a bit like watching a bad horror film, when you know it's not that scary but you can't help but jump. "I never knew why my mother left, but you know what? I'm suddenly starting to wonder, and Bianca? Yeah, when the hell did you start to worry about me and Bianca?"

"Since she made you look a dick." The man really did need a wider vocabulary.

"Is that what you're worried about? How I look?" Saul gave a short laugh, and shook his head. "Are you sure it wasn't all that money disappearing that bothered you? Or was it the fact she hated you anyway? Eh? What was it, really? What scares you most, Dad—the fact that I might look a fool, or the fact that I might actually work things out better than you did?"

"Grow up. Pussy has only one purpose, son, and the sooner you work that one out the better."

Roisin could almost feel her toes curl up; she held her breath, just waiting for the explosion. But it never came. Instead there was a soft, low laugh that was dangerous enough to tickle the hairs on the back of her neck.

"If you could only hear yourself. You know what? I felt sorry for you, but I've just realized what a stupid twat I've been. I've made a deal with Roisin and there's fuck all you can do about it now, so just do what she said and bugger off before I forget you're just a sad old man and flatten you." He took a step nearer, and the older man finally took a half step back. "And Dad, don't you ever"—he held his mobile up, tapped it—"pull a stunt like that again, or that's it."

"That's it? That's what, Saul? Face it, you need me."

"Oh yeah? Or is it you that needs me, Dad? Piss off. Please? Just go before one of us does something we regret and don't you ever come back here. Never, you hear me?"

Martin Mathews appeared more disgruntled than worried, and he was glaring at her breasts again, which she reckoned were probably heaving, with hard nipples thrown in for good measure. She was sure he was about to make some crude comment, but something changed his mind and, after a brief stare in her direction, he stomped off, leaving her with his son. The man she'd trusted, the man she didn't mind ogling her, and undressing her more than mentally. The man who'd taken her to be an idiot, which would have been okay if she hadn't been one.

<center>~~~</center>

He pulled the stable door open, the safe barrier that had stood between her and his father, and she suddenly felt exposed. "I thought that was who you'd had to rush off to meet, your dad?"

"So did I. It was a trick." He was rocking slightly on his heels, watching her as though he expected her to make a bolt for the door.

"But you said it was urgent, you said he'd rung and you had to go." She was trying to stay calm, trying not to launch into attack mode, but her heart was hammering in her ears and she felt like someone had wound her up and pointed her in the right direction. Which they had.

"He had rung, and it was urgent." He glared as though she was missing something. "Then he sent a text for good measure too, which should have warned me something was up. The bastard said he'd been arrested again." She raised an eyebrow; "again" made it sound like a bad habit. "Don't give me that look; from where I'm standing your family aren't exactly angels either."

"They don't get arrested; well, not as far as I know." But what did she know? She swallowed away the dryness in her throat; maybe he knew more about her family than he was letting on. No, she was being paranoid. It was a throwaway comment, that was all.

"Yeah, well, last time he'd threatened a client and they called the police. I'm sure the idiot thinks he's England's answer to the mafia sometimes, but he's living in a bloody seventies cop show if you ask me." She tried not to smile at the rasp in his voice. And then he looked up at her. Dark, angry eyes that seemed to be mirroring a frustration she hadn't a hope in hell of understanding. "The whole fiasco lost us a huge contract; it took months to put things back on an even keel." He shrugged, as though trying to dismiss the heavy frown. "He rang to tell me he'd done it again. He knew it was the one way of getting me to rush away from here."

"So you fell for it."

"I got twenty miles down the road and something just felt wrong, so I rang our solicitor who didn't have a clue what I was talking about. So—"

"So you came back?"

"I figured he was up to something, I just didn't know what."

"Why does he want me out?"

"You want a list? Let's see, you're one of them—" He counted off on his fingers. "Inherited wealth, and he hates that; you're a woman, which makes you manipulative and greedy; you've roots and so you must be sneering at self-made people like us; and you're stopping me getting on with making the maximum money I can out of this place. Enough to be going on with?"

"And you never told him about our deal?"

"He's not my keeper."

"And you lied to me about Toby?" She'd tried to keep her tone on the same conversational note, but she could hear the slight crack as she let the pitchfork drop with a metallic clank into the wheelbarrow. He'd lied. Whatever he said now, he'd lied.

"What are you talking about? I didn't lie." He shifted his weight. "Okay, I might not have told you everything, but I didn't lie."

It was biting at her and she couldn't help it. Even though she didn't really want him to confirm what his father had said, even though it was safer not to say it. "Why did you have to shag me, Saul? Tell me that. What was all that about? You already had the place, all you had to do was throw me out, not shag me like I'm some bonus part of the deal."

"Oh, for fuck's sake, you were never some perk of the job, Roisin. You know you weren't." He shoved his hands deep into his pockets as though he didn't trust to have them loose. "And you know I can't throw you out even if I don't understand why it's so important for you to stay."

"I don't know anything, Saul. I'm not even your type. Am I just filling a space like I was for Toby, eh? What am I, a challenge? I'm not going to let you just use me."

"You're certainly a challenge, but you're talking crap. And how the fuck do you work out I'm using you? Isn't it more likely the other way around? That you're keeping me happy, keeping me dangling on a string so you don't have to go, eh? Keeping me happy while you screw around with James."

"Piss off. Offering to share the premises was all your idea, not mine, and you knew James came as part of it. You just never thought I'd go along with it, did you? You never thought I'd do it." The words were out before she realized what she was saying. Before she'd registered that it was the truth, what it all came down to. She leaned back against the stable wall, knowing her legs were trembling. He'd never thought she'd do it. She was supposed to give in, give up, and walk away.

"No." He looked straight at her then, and she knew this bit wasn't a lie. "No, Roisin, I never thought you'd have the balls. I made the offer to make myself feel better because I thought you didn't deserve to be in the shit like you were. I wanted it to be your decision to give up. Was that what you wanted to hear me say?"

"Well I'm not going to." Mr. Shagathon might have made her insides melt, but her mind hadn't quite turned to mush yet; she was still capable of doing something for herself. "I'm not giving up." Her nails dug painfully into the palms of her hands.

"I gathered that." He picked up a piece of straw, twisted it around his finger, and leaned back against the doorjamb as though he wanted something else to take his weight. "And you know what, I'm glad. I don't want you to give up." It could have been a sigh, she wasn't sure, but she could see he was thinking of going. "I don't, and that's the truth, for what it's worth."

"Saul." He had levered himself away, was going; she just knew he was off and something twisting in her chest was telling her not to let him. She had to talk. "Does your dad hate all women, or just ones like me?"

He shrugged, relaxed back a whisper of an inch. "I never realized he did until just now. Funny, isn't it, how you never really look at your parents as people who can do wrong?"

"Dead funny." Dads and doing wrong went together perfectly, as far as she was concerned. Except maybe they hadn't a long time ago, when she was young, when she was still into hero worship. Until her father had gone and shattered the mirror of self-deception. "Why is he like that, so…"

"Bitter?" His face twisted. "Dad was brought up in an orphanage, but he worked bloody hard to make something of himself. When he met my mom he thought he'd finally made the grade, gone from barrow boy to Lord Muck. She was rich, seriously rich, and all of it inherited, so she was the total opposite of Dad. Then she walked out on him, and all of a sudden he hated everything she stood for; she left us for someone even richer than she was. He wasn't good enough and nor was I, and that hurts when you're little, you know, finding out you're not good enough even for your own mom. So we forgot her. Dad looked after me, got me a job on a building site with him as soon as I was old enough. I bought a house as soon as I could and we did it up together, sold it on, and that was the start of the business. I dunno, maybe she left because of the giant chip he had on his shoulder. Maybe you're right; maybe he just doesn't like women."

"But he liked Bianca." He liked Saul's ex-wife, his spanking buddy.

"Shit, no. They hated each other. But he hated me even more for throwing her out."

"That's a strange thing to say."

"He's a strange man." He shook his head; he was looking straight at her but she knew he wasn't seeing her at all. "Bianca was well off, had connections in all kinds of places. I didn't realize when I first met her but"—he looked wry—"I guess she met most of them playing Dungeons and Dragons."

"What is that supposed to mean?"

"If you don't know then you shouldn't be asking. Anyway, she had friends, contacts, and it wasn't long before we were making money faster than we ever had, but when she went so did the work. We were on the verge of signing a really big contract, and when we lost it, it nearly bankrupted us." He shrugged, and his eyes focused back on her. "All I had to do was keep it together one more week and it would have been sorted."

"But you couldn't?"

"Nope. Fucked up my marriage and my company just like that." He snapped his fingers and laughed, but there wasn't a trace of humor in the brown eyes. "So I deserve some of the aggravation he throws my way."

"Why?" She whispered it because she knew she shouldn't ask, but she had to know.

"Why did I throw her out? Because..." She watched his Adam's apple move convulsively, watched as his hand rifled through his hair. "Because she killed my child." There was a tic in his jaw that she wanted to reach out and touch, but she just held her breath and daren't move. "I didn't even know she was pregnant. She aborted it and told me purely as an explanation when I asked why she wasn't hungry."

She felt her stomach lurch. "Oh God, oh, I'm so—"

"Don't." The glare stopped her dead. "It was a long time ago and we would have made shitty parents anyway."

"But to—"

"And I guess it wasn't much worse than what my mother did to me."

"You can't say that." She tried to ignore the look. "How can you say that when you don't know what happened? Have you ever even asked your mom?" She wanted to touch him, to help him, to make everything better. But she couldn't. She didn't know how to. He was telling her things, but he wasn't sharing; he was farther away than he'd ever been.

"Nope, I haven't a clue where she is; she just packed and went, whoosh, right out of my life."

"Are you sure? Saul, not many women can just pack and go

and leave their kids." He'd set his chin again and the gap was widening; she was making it worse. He had his "don't touch" sign erected and, all of a sudden, they seemed to be on quicksand.

"It doesn't matter." He ran his hand through his hair in that familiar gesture. "I only told you because you asked why my father hated women."

"I think it probably does matter, though."

"Drop it, Roisin. It's not your problem."

"And never questioning it works for you, does it? Never asking yourself if it was maybe your dad at fault, not the fact of where he came from but that he was too busy looking after himself and your mother couldn't cope with it anymore. It's not easy staying with someone when you're struggling, but it's bloody impossible if you know they don't even love you."

"Yeah, and how would you know what he's like?"

"I've got eyes, Saul, and you know what? You're going to end up just as bitter and twisted as him if you're not careful."

"You don't know anything about me. You were brought up with money, a loving family, everything you ever wanted so how can you possibly understand my dad or me?"

It pulled her up short. "No, I don't, do I? And you don't know anything about me and"—he was going to go, she just knew he was going to go—"what did he mean, make opportunities?" She had to know everything before he walked.

"I'm not discussing this anymore."

"Saul, tell me, I need to know. You've got to tell me. What did he mean?"

"Got to? I don't have to tell you anything." He was staring at her, and suddenly she felt like she didn't know him at all.

"You've got ten seconds to tell me or this finishes, now."

"Finishes?" He shook his head slowly, fixed her with a gaze that made everything suddenly so final. "Who said anything ever started? No one gives me an ultimatum, darling. No one."

Chapter 11

THE WHISKEY SHOULD HAVE hit the spot, but it didn't. It didn't give him a warm, fuzzy feeling; it just left a hot, acrid streak that melted to nothing. Saul took another long swallow. He felt like total, absolute shit. Where had all that starting and finishing crap come from? She'd pushed him too far; after all, he'd been more than fair. She should have been bloody grateful; he'd given her a way out of the mess. A way they could both be happy with, but she just wanted more, didn't she? He'd been fair; he'd played by the rules even if they weren't rules that people like her agreed with. He was in there to win, to make money, to prove to himself and his dad that he could still do it. Prove he could use his head, not his heart.

Shit. He poured another good slug, picked up the glass again, and then set it down with a hard clunk. How much of this was just about doing what his dad wanted, about making sure he was happy and wouldn't leave him like his mom did? If he was honest with himself, he'd offered Roisin a job and a tenancy because he felt guilty about what he'd done, and he'd also done it because he wanted to see her writhing underneath him, begging for more. He couldn't ignore that bit; he'd wanted to see her. Full stop.

But he should have seen it coming, because he'd known deep down that if she found out what he'd done, he'd be history. So he'd saved himself from having to tell her by being a shit. By pretending nothing had happened between them. Even though she was the only person he'd ever told the full Bianca story to. The only person he'd trusted. Which meant something had started.

He grabbed his tablet off the floor; he'd email her and explain. He couldn't beg, he couldn't try and change her mind, but he could set things straight, give her what she wanted. The answers. Let her know she hadn't been duped, that she hadn't been just another careless shag. It had been right girl, but wrong time, wrong place.

He wasn't even sure he remembered her email address, but the second he logged in his eyes were pulled instinctively to one unread email, glaring out at him from the top of the list like some threat that was better ignored, except he knew that nothing went away when you ignored it. And he didn't want her to go away. Even though he wasn't quite ready to let himself question why.

Saul,

I don't really know what I'm trying to say here or why I'm bothering, but I couldn't sleep because I knew I had to say something and I can't say it so I'm writing it. I guess we all have problems but at least yours are still there to face.

I told you Dad was dead—well, he shot himself in the head. He was a loser but I still loved him, which I hadn't really thought about until I was shouting at you today. He'd inherited money, lots I suppose, though I never really thought about it. And you're right, I had everything when I was a kid, but somewhere along the line he made bad mistakes and once he started it was like his luck had turned rotten and it just got worse and worse. He lost it on deals, but then he just kept on spending on drink and women because he couldn't face up to Mom anymore. Dads are supposed to be superhuman, aren't they? They don't make mistakes and they're supposed to be able to handle everything. He was too old-fashioned to discuss it with anyone, or admit he'd made a mistake, so he just carried on trying to sort things his way. Still awake?

Yeah, still awake, Miss Bossy. How can I not be when you're making me feel even guiltier than I did before? He shifted uneasily in his chair; he'd never asked her about her family, her problems. He'd just assumed that it all started and stopped with Toby. He'd never given her a chance to say otherwise. Though he doubted she'd have told him anyway. Was she only telling him now because she thought she'd never have to look at his ugly face again?

We had a big house a few miles away, and he burned it down, with Mom and my sister still inside. The inquiry said he probably drugged them, and the dogs, but we'll never know for sure. Then he drank a bottle of whiskey and shot himself. He left a note for me and my brother and he blamed people like you, City men in suits who didn't give a damn, vultures circling for the kill, he said, and today I felt like maybe you've proved him right. Everything was someone else's fault, which I know it wasn't really, but there you go.

Anyhow, that's when Toby asked me to marry him, because we'd been dating and he promised Dad he'd look after me. Dad had even signed this place, my place, over to him, though it was probably more as a tax dodge than because he liked him. I should have said no, he should have said no, but it was the last thing Dad asked him to do, so I suppose he tried.

So that's my sob story, and it's why people like me don't trust people like you, and it's why I tried so hard to hang on to this place and stay here. But hey, guess what? You've just made me realize I don't need it anymore. I don't need to hang on to the past because I can't get away from it even if I want to.

I don't want charity from you or your dad. You want this place? Well, it's all yours—bring in the bulldozers, baby. I guess working with you was always a no-no, but I don't want anything from you now. Not even answers. Give me a month to sell the horses. It's probably best if I just close the door behind me and leave the key, isn't it?

It was fun.

Roisin x

P.S. I still think you should talk to your mom.

He should have known when she'd thrown that ultimatum at him that she'd stick by it. When he'd first seen her in that bar and put a hand on her knee she'd not backed down, even though she seemed so not the type. When he'd come up with his cock-eyed proposition and she should have run a mile, she'd called his bluff and jumped in feetfirst. He swirled the whiskey in the glass, then put it down again. He didn't want her to close the door and leave the key.

He emailed his response almost without thinking about it.

Roisin, I thought we had a deal? You signed a contract. This isn't charity. This is you working for me, remember? Saul.
P.S. Stop telling me what to do!

The reply came back almost instantly.

I just quit. You said you'd changed your mind, well, I've changed mine.
P.S. Someone needs to tell you.

The response he fired off was brief.

I never had you down as a quitting type. And who's going to boss me about if you bugger off and leave me? Saul.

Roisin's reply was even briefer.

I never had you down as a lying type. You'll find someone else to do it.

That stung.

Ouch. No one could do it quite like you.

He hit Enter, refreshed the page impatiently when there wasn't an immediate response, and fought the urge to pick up his mobile.

I never got any of this, why you gave me a job, and I just decided that from now on what I don't get I don't put up with.

He could just imagine her sitting there on the bed, biting her lip, and he wanted to see it again.

I'm not a lying type, or a long email type, but hang on and I'll send one...And don't argue or go to sleep.

He pressed Send, finished the whiskey, and poured another.

I don't know what Dad said to you, but I never meant to mislead you, Roisin. I never meant to fall for you either. I came to your place to finish off a job. Yeah, Dad was right, we'd spent time creating an opportunity, and it makes me feel like shit because you never deserved it. Your husband had been digging himself into a hole for a long time; he liked taking a risk but he wasn't good at it. Not many people are; that's why the bookies are always the winners.

So we watched and we didn't help him out, we passed him a bigger shovel. We made him an offer months ago for the place which would have gotten him out of trouble, but he was sure if he carried on gambling he'd sort it. Then he got to the point where he had no choice because we made sure all the debts were called in at the same time. That's what making opportunities involves. The best bit for Dad was always closing the deal, watching the mighty fall, maybe his way of making even with Mom, or maybe that's reading too much into it, too deep for him. Maybe he is just one of your City men, except he's probably more just the shark. But I suppose like you love your dad, I still love mine. Toby should have told you, and you should have moved out and handed over the keys well before he died, but he kept stalling and I don't know why, but I let him. And you know what, girl? I'm glad, because I wouldn't have met you otherwise.

Fun isn't the right word. Don't sell the horses. X

His finger hovered over the Send button. He'd been soft before, he'd told Bianca how he felt and sworn he'd give her a happy ever after, and he wasn't sure he could do it again. But he couldn't walk away either. Roisin had probably been right; she knew she couldn't escape her past but she could move on; she didn't have to hang on to anything. Like he'd been hanging on to every bad bit of his car-crash marriage, hanging on to something he really should have let go of. Just like his dad had.

—⁓—

Roisin stared at the words; she should hate him. Except Toby had pressed the self-destruct button a long time ago, and even without help he would have gotten there in the end.

So what is the right word?

Shit, the sudden ring of her mobile phone nearly made her jump off the bed. She'd been concentrating so hard on her laptop, willing each email to pop up in her inbox. She pressed the Receive Call button as she picked it up; she couldn't have done anything else right now even if she'd had a list of all the reasons not to in front of her. He didn't even wait for her to say anything.

"Totally mind-blowing?"

"That's two words."

"Fucking fantastic?"

"Nope. You really can't count, can you?"

"Amazing."

"Better."

"I never meant to mix business and pleasure, Roisin." The way his soft tones sent a swirl of warmth straight to the base of her stomach made her hug her knees up to her chest. "And I'm so sorry about your family, everything."

"Don't. Why've you rung?"

"My internet went down. I couldn't email."

"Really?"

"No. Not really." His sigh traveled straight down from her ear to somewhere deep inside her. "I just thought I might need an excuse."

"So the shagging wasn't to soften me up? Or because you felt sorry for me or…"

"The shagging was because I had this deep, irresistible urge to rip your panties off the moment I saw you."

"The first moment?"

"Yup, when you stood there with your glass of wine behind that bar looking all prim and proper I just wanted to leap over and shag you senseless."

"Really?" She wriggled deeper onto the bed, kicked the laptop to the bottom.

"When I touched you I thought my cock was going to explode. I wanted to slip my hand up your thigh to check your pussy was as wet as I knew it would be."

"You thought all that while I was pouring you a pint?" The warm feeling was spreading through her body.

"Mmm, it got worse once I'd touched your knee, and now I'm imagining you lying in bed."

"Really?" She should be able to say something more intelligent, something sexy, just anything. She wriggled self-consciously, feeling like he was watching her.

"You're lying naked on your crisp white cotton sheets and I'm lying next to you."

"Mmm." Intelligent words, it seemed, had now run out altogether. "Well, actually I've got a nightdress on."

She heard a groan. "That makes it even better." There was a long silence. "Okay, I've gotten over my nightdress fantasy, for now." She felt a smile twitch the corners of her mouth. "I want to kiss you, Roisin. I love the feel of your soft lips under mine, the way you softly part them so that I can slip my tongue inside and taste you." She could feel her lips parting at his words. "That first kiss did something strange to me. It wasn't just a kiss; it was a promise." The deep, dark words seeped into her, sending spears of longing between her thighs. "When we were standing in that dark spot against the wall, all I could see was a shadow, tempting me closer. You were tempting me, you were asking me to take control, to pin you against that wall, weren't you? Tell me, please, Roisin. I want to hear you say it."

"Yes." She snaked her tongue over dry lips. "I wanted you to kiss me; I needed to feel your hands on me."

"You tasted so sweet, and you were wrapping your fingers tight in my hair, and all I could think of was how it would feel to have your fingers wrapped around my cock. I slipped my fingers inside you, and you were so wet I wanted to have you there and then; that sweet pussy of yours was made for my fingers, and you rode them, rode and gripped them, riding my hand. As I sucked your tongue I could taste you, and it was almost like I was sucking that tender, swollen clit and tasting your juices. You know how hard I was for you then, Roisin?"

"I know." She forced the words out, rocking her hips as the ache grew between her thighs.

"I'm hard for you now, Roisin, are you wet for me? Is this turning you on? Touch yourself; touch that sweet, wet pussy for me."

How could he do this to her? How could just the sound of his voice whispering dirty things in her ear be making her so damp, so hot that she felt like a gooey, needy mass of want? A rush of juices spilled onto her hand as she teased her swollen labia apart with the tip of her finger, a wave of pleasure instantly rippling through her, and she moaned with pleasure, sliding her finger farther inside, rubbing her thumb gently against her swollen clit.

"Do you remember what happened next?"

Her knees dropped wider apart. "Tell me." She slowly slipped the finger deeper into her moist cunt, closing her eyes, resisting the urge to drop the mobile.

"I had you on those stairs; I couldn't resist that smell of you as you ran up. You were flicking your skirt so that I could see your panties, and I could still remember the taste of you on my fingers, and I needed to taste you properly. I want my tongue inside you now, Roisin, want to slip inside you, lap up your juices. Lick your fingers for me, taste what I tasted, and pretend I'm doing it. Lick them for me."

She groaned. "I can't."

"Please, Roisin."

Shit. She rocked her hips, curling her finger against her G-spot, feeling the quiver of new sensation. The groan in her ear made her pussy clench. "I want to hear you come for me. How many fingers have you got inside? Two?"

She gasped. "One."

"Put two in, slide two in nice and deep. Oh God, I can hear you; you're so slick, so fucking wet I can hear you sliding in and out."

"What are you doing?"

"I've got my fingers curled around my cock for you, and all I can think of is your mouth on me. I love the way you suck me." She could hear the sound of his hand sliding up and down his shaft and she shut her eyes, could picture him so clearly he could be there with her.

"I'm so close, darling; I want us to come together." His voice had a rasp to it now, a rasp that was making her push her fingers harder, faster. His breath was quickening to match hers, echoing in her ear as though he was right there in the room, watching her, his hard cock throbbing. She wanted to see him come, wanted to see his sperm shoot out; see what it was like as it shot deep inside her. "Rub your clit with your other hand, fuck yourself."

The phone dropped on the pillow next to her, his harsh, unsteady breathing still in her ear. The coolness of her touch hit her clit, and her pussy closed around her fingers. "Ouu shit." A flutter of soft spasms was building high inside her. "I want to see you come, Saul."

He groaned. "Do you want me to come over your stomach while my fingers are playing in your pussy?" His voice was uneven, breaking along with his self-control.

"I want to see you shooting out, imagine how it feels when you do that inside me."

"Shit, Roisin, I can't hold back much longer."

Nor could she. The thought of his hot sperm hitting her stomach, of the smell of him all around her, was making her fingers work harder and faster.

"I'm fucking you with one hand, fucking you as fast as I'm tugging at this big cock. Can you imagine that?"

She could, and she was coming, a shattering spread of feeling shooting around her fingers, filling her pussy as bright pinpricks of light lit the back of her eyelids, her breath uneven as her body rocked with the rolling wave inside her. She could hear his gasp, his matching groan, could picture him coming all over her as her cunt still fluttered around her fingers.

"You're going to be the death of me, girl." His voice was still unsteady and she rolled onto her side, nearer to the phone, not wanting to reach out and pick it up.

"Mmm."

"You've still got your fingers in there, haven't you?"

"Mmm, I can't move."

"If I was there I'd move you, flip you onto your stomach, and…"

"Oh, stop it, Saul. I can't. Don't set me off again." Okay, she only half meant it, but she felt so bloody wiped out. His laugh seemed to reach down, making her fingers twitch, and she pulled her damp hand from between her thighs.

"You're a bad girl."

"You're badder." She could hardly talk, the words slipping from her mouth just to keep him there because she didn't want him to go yet.

"That isn't a word." His voice was soft; she pulled the mobile tighter to her ear, wanting to let that deep rumble of his resonate inside her. "You're tired, you need to sleep, darling."

"Mmm, I do."

"I'll come tomorrow, we'll talk, okay?"

"What we gonna talk about now?" She stifled a yawn, spreading her leg over the spot where his body should be, pulling the pillow he'd used closer. "But you'll come anyway?"

"Oh, you won't be able to keep me away. How about you make me lunch? I've got an appointment first thing."

"Mmm." A trace of his musky scent reached out to her and she pulled the pillow closer, letting the woody, citrus scents seep into her mind.

"Night darling, sweet dreams."

And it was almost as though he was there, almost as though he was kissing her on the neck and the warmth of his body was wrapped around hers. Almost.

Chapter 12

THE COLD DAMPNESS OF early morning wrapped around her as she saddled up the horse. This had always been her favorite time of the day to ride. Just as the birds were waking, and the rest of the world was still asleep. It was fresh, virgin air that took your breath away, that carried the promise of the new day.

She pulled the girth up another notch and sprang up onto the saddle, gathering the reins decisively. The horse sensed her impatience, breaking into a trot the moment his hooves hit the dew-sodden grass. She sat deep and he danced sideways briefly before rocking into a canter that turned to a gallop as she eased her weight forward. They cleared the first fence effortlessly, the horse settling into a steady rhythm that she could lose herself in. She knew this land like the back of her hand, had ridden here more days than she could remember, but she'd almost forgotten what it was like to let go, hand over control, and let the horse take her. It seemed like a lifetime since the last time she had done this. In those days it had been simple, easy to just jump onto the ponies bareback with only a halter rope in her hand and trust them to take control, take care of her.

Her eyes smarted from the cold air and her hair whipped across her face, but she pushed on, taking the final fence before slowing to turn on to the track that led down to the river. The horse dropped into a steady jog. She'd told Saul she could walk away from all this, that she'd close the door and leave the keys behind and she had thought she could. But this place was her heart—it was in her blood—and walking away would be leaving more than memories behind; it would be leaving a part of herself that she was afraid she might never find again. She slipped from the saddle as the ground became uneven when they neared the edge of the water, let the horse pick his way down the bank.

"What you doing down here so early?"

The soft voice made her jump, then he stepped away from the tree he'd been leaning against. James. Doing his big cat act.

She let her eyes drift over him, gave herself time to gather her thoughts back from where they'd strayed. He was lean; almost sleek she'd say, if you could apply that word to a man. Every part of him toned and defined, but not in a bulky, muscle-bound way, more sinew and quiet strength. "I could ask you the same; I'm not used to having company at this time of day."

"Don't worry, I'm not stalking you." He grinned as heat flooded her face, capable of reading her mind as well as her body, it seemed.

"I like to ride in the morning. It helps me think." She sat down on the bank, half expecting him to sit next to her, but he didn't. "Get my head straight."

"He wouldn't have asked me to join the two of you if he didn't really care, you know." Which wasn't at all what she expected him to say. "I think he was digging for answers of his own before he dared admit to himself what was going on."

"Oh."

"With Bianca he never even stopped to question it. He didn't care enough."

"Maybe it was just because he was younger, cared more?"

"Nope." He took a step nearer the water. "They were completely wrong for each other; it just took a lot of banging his head against the wall before he'd admit it. He can be a bloody stubborn git, you know."

"Oh, I think I already worked that one out."

"Has he asked you to stay?"

"Yeah." She studied her fingernails.

"Then I'd give it a whirl, babe. Nothing comes with a guarantee but you have to try it and see sometimes."

She laughed, looked up, and he was actually smiling. Or at least his hard eyes were crinkling around the edges, and the corners of his mouth were tipped up. "You like him, don't you, James?"

"There's a lot to like, if you give him a chance. Maybe you could even persuade him to like himself again."

"What does that mean?"

"Whatever you want, darling. He's tried to make things right, he's decent."

"I know."

"Not that he ever really did anything wrong."

"Hmm, maybe."

"Gotta be worth something, eh?" He took a step back up the bank, put a hand out, and hauled her to her feet. "And besides, if you go I might be out of a job." He winked, then his hard lips brushed against hers and he strode up the bank as smooth as you like, his stride eating up the ground.

Shit, he probably was a panther. No one crept up on her like that without her noticing. What did they call them—shape-shifters? She shook her head and grinned to herself, then twitched the horse's reins. He reluctantly lifted his head from the grass he'd been picking at and took a step closer. She led him up the bank, paused for a second before mounting, and looked around. No sign of James at all. She left her reins long, and nudged the horse into a loping stride. Maybe she'd just imagined the whole conversation. Except her lips could still feel the dry brush of his mouth.

She'd wanted Saul gone, had wanted him out of her life when she'd found out there was more to this than he'd admitted to. But maybe he hadn't lied; maybe, like James said, he had tried to make things right, things that had never really been his fault in the first place. Maybe she'd been at fault pushing him like that; maybe she didn't blame him for storming off. He wasn't the type of man to be bullied and she had known that, which could be why she'd pushed him that bit too far, to make him go. And then she didn't have to make the decision herself. But he'd known where Toby was heading so long ago, and just watched. He'd taken advantage of the fact that her husband was a weak-willed fool. But then Toby was no better, she supposed; he'd been betting to win, hadn't he? He'd been greedy, but he just hadn't been clever enough. Not like Saul.

He'd told her not to go—not asked, told. She grinned. Did the man ever ask for anything? She didn't want to go, and she didn't want him to go either, if she was honest. She felt safe when he was there, like there was something to lean on. Something solid.

He wanted her to stay, and everything in her was screaming yes, except for that tiny bit of her brain that was common sense. The bit that told her she was fighting a battle she could never win, that maybe she'd finally met a man she felt she could rely on, but he was a man who wasn't in a place where he could make promises. Who couldn't hang around.

She knew she couldn't resist him; last night proved that. Even two-hundred-odd miles away he still had the power to turn her on, could have her whole body humming, which had to mean something, didn't it? Maybe she did have to try it and see. If he still wanted her to. And she wouldn't know that until he turned up for his lunch.

She gathered up the reins and nudged the horse with her heels. One last gallop before she headed home. One last adrenaline rush to clear the cobwebs from her head, then she'd find out if she had it in her to give it a whirl.

—⁓—

"I unloaded all that stuff on you last night thinking I'd never see you again." She pushed a mug of coffee across the table, wishing he'd sit down and stop that "looking at her" thing he did. He wasn't supposed to be back yet and the hat hair from riding, along with the gear, wasn't a good look. Or a good smell. And she didn't want to be faced with what she'd said in the emails. That was just awkward.

"I gathered that."

"So now it's a bit…" She paused. It was more than a bit; it was full-on embarrassing. Along with him knowing that last night she'd been finger-fucking for England. To put it crudely, which she didn't normally. "What?" He was looking at her in a way she wasn't sure she liked. As if he was reading her mind.

"You're thinking about last night, aren't you?" He grinned and took a step closer. "I like the thought of you getting all horny when I'm talking dirty to you."

"Stop it, Saul, I don't want…" What had she been about to say, that she didn't want it just to be about sex? But it was. And it was better that way. Not relying on someone, not putting all your eggs in one basket. She wouldn't be in this mess now if they hadn't all relied on her dad, if she hadn't relied on Toby.

"What don't you want?"

She didn't know.

"None of this is your fault, Roisin, you've just been unlucky."

"Oh yeah. Maybe I just need a break from all this, from all this shagging and then I can get my head straight."

He laughed, which wasn't what he was supposed to do. "How can shagging stop you thinking straight?"

She glared. "It does, stop laughing at me. You're in my space, in my head, and it confuses me, right?"

"I'm not in your head if it's just sex, Roisin."

He sat down, and he stopped looking at her and started to trace circles on the table with one finger. "I went to see my mother this morning."

"Your mom?" Well, that had effectively stopped her worrying about having him in her head. She sat down and stared at him, as though it might help. Which it didn't. She could ask what, why, when. Or she could keep quiet for once and bite her tongue and wish she could read his mind.

"I went to see my mother because some interfering busybody kept saying it was a good idea."

"Was it?" If she whispered it, then he could ignore her if he wanted.

"Dunno really. After you'd yelled at me—"

"I didn't."

"You did. After you yelled I slammed a few things around, then decided maybe I was missing a trick, maybe I better check the room out before I locked the door and threw away the key."

"One way of putting it, I suppose. You're a bit weird, you know."

"Says she." He grinned and suddenly it seemed a bit easier again. "And?"

"Ah, I was waiting for you to give in to nosiness again."

"You're so bloody annoying at times." Didn't he realize just how high on the patience scale this rated for her? She'd given him seconds—no, minutes—before prodding for an answer. He suddenly glanced up and for a second looked almost vulnerable, a weird mix of need and uncertainty that she hadn't seen before. "What was she like, Saul?"

"Nice enough." He gave her a warning look. "No fairy tale happy ever after, so don't even go there, but then she doesn't know me from Adam and this is a one-off, okay? But at least she agreed to talk to me." His hand stilled and he half smiled. "I don't suppose you ever understand anybody else's relationship, do you? But she didn't have a go at him like I thought she might. Apparently Dad told her one too many times that a woman should know her place. Figures, doesn't it?" She reached over and put a hand over his own large one that was still tracing ever-decreasing circles on the table top. He didn't move away, at least. "She found out he was investing their money in businesses she knew nothing about and she blew a fuse. I think she's quite conservative, really, and it bothered her. Anyway, it turned into a shouting match and he called her posh totty."

Roisin felt herself cringe; she couldn't help it. Seemed he hadn't changed over the years.

"I know." Saul laughed. "She told me she called him a second-hand car salesman and he went ballistic. I suspect things were thrown." He grinned, a grin that reached right into his eyes.

Ah, so it wasn't just her who had thought that way.

"And she walked out the next day. She knew he'd object and, however many times she told him she would, he didn't believe it would happen so she proved it. I think she felt like she was just there as arm candy and a source of money, which wasn't her at all. I think she's quite smart." He turned his hand over, his fingers curled up and entwined with hers. Took a deep breath. "The solicitors said I was old enough to have an opinion on who I lived with, and I kept insisting on being with Dad. I don't even remember that bit. She was advised to settle on access, as if it went to court she was likely to lose, especially as he threatened he'd use abandonment. She worked abroad quite a lot at the time, apparently, and she said she thought she was doing what was best for me. Keeping it calm and as friendly as she could."

"Oh."

"I told her I wished she'd fought for me." His fingers tightened around hers. "And she said once she'd realized she'd made a mistake it was too late; I told her I didn't want to see her. Or rather, Dad did."

"And she believed him?"

He shrugged. "She thought it was better if it was just her suffering, as long as I was happy and doing what I wanted."

"You didn't see her at all?"

"Nope, he wouldn't let her, kept insisting I didn't want to see her. She said she just kept an eye on me over the years. So she knew a hell of a lot more about me than I did about her."

"Which is the right way; she should know about you."

"If you say so, dear."

"Ha, nice of you to say it."

"You might never hear it again." He grinned, then instantly sobered again. "She never had any more children though, didn't even remarry until a few years ago, and all the time I thought she'd left us for someone else."

"Ah."

He softened his grip slightly on her fingers and she suddenly realized she was clutching his hand. She pulled free; she was being silly, hanging on when all he'd done was come to explain, to tell her he'd finally done what he should have done years ago. It didn't change anything between them. What he wanted, what she wanted. They'd both be repeating mistakes they'd made in the past.

"I want you to stay, Roisin. Please. I want you to stay and find out if it is just about sex."

"But you said…"

"Me and Bianca were a mistake. We met when we were both drunk, when she was being the party animal she is and I was just bouncing from one bed to another. She thought I was a challenge and I thought she was a keeper."

"But you loved her."

"I thought so, for a while. She gave me something none of the others ever had, and I made the mistake of thinking she'd slow down but she just wanted to crash and burn. I couldn't accept that I wasn't enough for her, that any high would never be high enough. I was too proud to admit it and let go, so she tortured me until I finally let her off the leash."

"What if I'm not enough for you, Saul? I'm boring, normal, one of those spoiled girls with a rich daddy, aren't I? Your dad hates me."

"You're more than enough for any man, Roisin, and you don't

have a rich daddy. Which is a shame, actually, but I suppose I can live with it." She went to slap him and, as usual, he fielded it, caught her hand, pulled it to his lips, and kissed the tip of each finger.

"Your dad hates me."

He gently nipped the tip of her first finger. "I don't really care; I've spent far too much time trying to prove to Dad that I'm him in miniature, and who really wants to be a mini me? He's made mistakes, I've made mistakes, I guess we all do. But I don't intend making one now." His mouth moved on to the next finger.

"Meaning?"

"Letting you squirm your way out of this. Anyway, I don't think he does hate you; he hates what you might be, not what you are." Slowly ran his tongue up her thumb.

"And what might I be? Another Bianca?"

"You're obsessed with that woman, worse than me. You're nothing like her, believe me. The only thing you've got in common is your gender, and with her I was even starting to wonder about that." He grinned at her. "She was rich, but you're not even that, are you, honey?"

"Ouu, nasty."

"But true. She was new money, brash, grasping, and greedy. Rich, but certainly no lady."

"And what am I?"

"Aha, who's fishing for compliments now? I guess you're more like Mom." He pulled her onto his lap.

"Your dad hates her too."

"But I don't think he always did, do you?" His voice was soft. "You're a lady, Roisin." He nuzzled her neck, sending a rush of goose bumps right down to her toes.

"I don't want to rely on anyone ever again."

"I know."

"I want to know I'll be okay."

"You'll always be okay, Roisin; you're just made that way." His teeth traced their way down her neck.

"And I want to be able to keep the agreement with Dan and Marie."

"Okay." It was slightly drawn out, slightly dubious.

"And I want to get involved and play a little." He paused, his lips resting just where her shoulder met her neck.

"Okay." More drawn out. "Just a little?"

"Just a little, Saul. And"—he was giving her the evil eye now—"I want to get a shower before we do any more talking. In fact, we've done too much talking."

"You do stink; I didn't really like to say anything."

"I don't stink, and if I do it's a stink you need to get used to."

"Look, believe me, it's not. In fact, I'm going to run you a bath."

"But we've not even eaten yet."

He laughed, and made a sudden lunge that caught her completely unawares, sweeping her off her feet and over his shoulder.

"Ouu, fireman too are we now?"

"Anything for you. Shall I put the uniform on?"

"Oh yes, please." A sharp hand came down on her bum and she squealed and kicked, but he was already heading up the stairs, carrying her effortlessly.

⌁

"Warm enough?"

"Mmm."

The way he was soaping her boobs it wouldn't have mattered what temperature the water was. His hand moved lower, slipped between her thighs.

"So you're going to stay and work for me?"

"With you." His finger played with the swollen lips of her pussy and she felt the moan build up in her chest.

"With me. Your choice." He slipped his finger deep inside, all the way to the knuckle, and bent his head to her nipple at the same time, sucking gently, insistently so that a tug of need went all the way from his mouth through her body to his fingers. "Always your choice." She groaned, threading her fingers into his thick hair and pulling his head down harder. As she did, he pressed his thumb tight against her clit. "You can say stop anytime you like and I'll go." He nibbled, sending an electric shock straight from her nipple to her clit, then rubbed a firm thumb over the swollen nub until she was sure she was going to scream.

"Oh fuck, don't stop."

"I meant everything, not this; no way am I stopping this."

"Fuck me, Saul, please." He screwed another finger into her, right to the knuckle, twisted his hand until she was panting, until her legs were sticking out of the bath because it was the only way she could open her hips any wider. Until a tidal wave of water shot out, drenching him.

"Why the hell did I ever think a bath was a good idea?" His voice was gruff, and then he was sliding three fingers into her in hard short bursts that had her body sliding from one end of the bath to the other. She reached behind her, trying to grasp the taps, and then it didn't matter; the orgasm was racing through her body and she was tipping her hips up, curling her body, desperate to clutch every last bit of satisfaction from the fingers that were working her pussy.

"That was good."

"This is better." He'd gotten her out of the bath and thrown her on the bed almost before she realized, was stripping off his own clothes that were sopping wet, and then his body was over hers. "I just have to warn you, this is one time you better say stop now, 'cause there won't be a second chance."

God, she loved the way his voice broke when he was this randy, this on the edge. She swallowed. "No way am I saying stop."

He was in her, buried balls deep with one hard thrust that did make her scream, then several steady thrusts that turned it to a moan. She could feel it building again, feel the spasms that would get her there. Then he stopped, rolled over abruptly so she was on top.

"Fuck me, Roisin. I want you to do it, make me come. Please."

She pulled her feet up so she was perched over him and grinned as she reached out, his hands meeting hers. They locked hands, fingers entwined, arms stretched. And then she did exactly what he *wanted*. Her way.

Acknowledgments

To Elizabeth Coldwell and Hazel Cushion, without whom this book wouldn't exist.

Restless Spirit

by Sommer Marsden

Three men want her. Only one can truly claim her.

When Tuesday Cane inherits a cozy lake house, she's not expecting to find love as part of her legacy. But how can she choose between Aiden, the loyal and über-sexy handyman she's known for years; the charming and wealthy Reed Green, a former TV star; and the mysterious Shepherd Moore, an ex cage fighter.

The only way to know for sure is to try them all… Surrounded by so many interesting men and erotic temptations, Tuesday has no intention of committing. But deep down she longs for that special, soul-deep connection. Only, which man can entice this restless spirit into finally settling down?

What readers are saying:

"An intense emotional and sexual journey that is quite compelling." —Kathy

"One of the best adult/erotica books I have ever read. The characters are real and believable, and the sex scenes are absolutely scorching hot." —Rebecca

"Themes of domination and submission are fantastically well varied throughout the story… Realistic and relatable characters with steamy encounters at every turn." —Michelle

For more Xcite Books, visit:

www.sourcebooks.com

Control

by Charlotte Stein

Will she choose control or just let go?

When Madison Morris wanted to hire a shop assistant for her naughty little bookstore, she never dreamed she'd have two handsome men vying for the position—and a whole lot more. Does she choose dark and dangerous Andy with his sexy tattoos? Or quiet, serious Gabriel, whose lean physique and gentle touch tempt her more than she thought possible?

She loves the way Andy takes charge when it comes to sex. But the turmoil in Gabe's eyes hints at a deep well of complicated emotions locked inside. When the fun and games are over, only one man can have control of her heart.

What readers are saying:

"Forget *Fifty Shades of Grey*…take a look at this and see how long you can stay in control!"

"This is honest to God, hands down, the best erotic fiction I've ever read."

"Highly addictive!"

For more Xcite Books, visit:

www.sourcebooks.com

The Initiation of Ms. Holly

by k. d. grace

The stranger on the train

He came to her in the dark. She couldn't see him, but she could feel every inch of his body against hers in the most erotic encounter Rita Holly ever had. And now he's promising more…if she'll just follow him to an exclusive club where opulence and sex rule. She can have anything she's ever dreamed of—and more—but first she'll have to pass the club's initiation…

What readers are saying:

"After reading *Fifty Shades of Grey*, I didn't think I would find another book as well written, but then I read *The Initiation of Ms. Holly*, and I was immediately taken in. This book is sexy, erotic, and explosive. I didn't want to put it down." —Dani

"Very, very erotic and sizzling!!! Wow, I could not put it down." —Theresa

"Everything you want in a romantic, erotic, sexual novel." —Jean

"For a fast-paced read with enough twists and turns to keep the story fresh and entertaining, you couldn't ask for a better book." —Christine

For more Xcite Books, visit:

www.sourcebooks.com

Telling Tales

by Charlotte Stein

The only limit is their imagination.

Allie has held a torch for Wade since college. They were part of a writing group together, and everything about those days with him and their friends Kitty and Cameron fills her with longing. When their former professor leaves them his mansion in his will, it's a chance for them to reunite. But there's more than friendship bubbling beneath the surface.

As relationships are rekindled and secrets revealed, they indulge their most primal desires. With the stakes getting higher, Allie isn't quite sure who she wants…fun-loving Wade or quiet, restrained Cameron.

For more Xcite Books, visit:

www.sourcebooks.com

Substitute

by Isobel Rey

She's driven by his desire...

It took all of Alexia's courage to leave her abusive boyfriend and strike out on her own. When she lands a job at a glamorous sports agency, she thinks she finally has it made. But shy, blond, and beautiful, Alexia is totally unprepared for the fast sexual politics of rich men and ambitious women that is waiting for her.

Most of all, she is totally unprepared for her new boss, Nathan Fallon.

Nathan is an ex-Army officer, dazzling but damaged, who has risen to the top of the cutthroat world of sports agents. There is no one Alexia wants more, but a case of mistaken identity has Nathan believing she's given herself over to the advances of the office playboy. Desperate to win Nathan's respect, Alexia agrees to become his substitute personal assistant. It doesn't take long for the sparks to fly...and for Alexia to find herself enthralled by a man she cannot read and could never resist.

Praise for Xcite erotic romances:

"Brilliant. Couldn't put it down."

"If you enjoyed *Fifty Shades of Grey*, you will enjoy this!"

"All the fun AND a good story."

For more Xcite books, visit:

www.sourcebooks.com

About the Author

Zara Stoneley has been writing stories for just about as long as she's been reading them. She sold her first erotic novel to Xcite Books in 2012 and has since had her hot romances accepted by several publishers. Her stories have featured on romance and erotic bestseller lists in the U.S. and the UK.

Zara divides her time between a country cottage in the UK and a Barcelona apartment and loves her family, sexy high heels, sunshine, good food and wine, coffee, cats, horses, dogs, music, writing, and reading—but not necessarily in that order!

Find out more about Zara at www.zarastoneley.com.